He whispered
then and you

Then he kissed her like there was no tomorrow, because he knew there might not be. As honor-bound as he felt to help Macy now that he knew T.J. was his son, he was also sure that he was not cut out for family or civilian life.

She responded to him willingly, going up on tiptoe to continue the kiss. He slipped his hands beneath her buttocks and lifted her until her backside was on the edge of the counter and her legs were straddling his.

Macy shivered as the hard jut of his erection brushed the center of her, awakening a rush of desire that dragged a moan from her.

The sound penetrated the fog of want that had wrapped itself around them, tempering their kisses, and creating a short lull during which she managed to murmur softly, "I'm sorry. I should have told you about T.J."

Dear Reader,

It was a pleasure to work on THE COLTONS: FAMILY FIRST due to the amazing authors with whom I get to work and our great editor, Patience Smith.

Soldier's Secret Child was particularly interesting since it let me explore the dynamics of a very different family. Macy Ward is an empowered and independent woman who has coped with a number of life issues. From an unexpected pregnancy to the loss of her first husband, Macy has grown emotionally and defended her family in order to give her teenaged son the right values.

Fisher Yates is a hero in every sense of the word. A military man who understands the values of honor and responsibility, Fisher is also a devoted son and brother. He also respects what Macy is trying to do for her family, although he is still hurt by the way their relationship turned out. Despite this, when Macy and her son need him, he is there for them— proving that being a hero doesn't end on the fields of battle.

I hope you will love exploring not only their relationship, but the happiness that love can bring to Macy, Fisher and their son, T.J.

Finally, I want to thank all the real-life heroes of the military—the men, women and their families who serve and sacrifice so that we all can enjoy the gift of Liberty.

Caridad Piñeiro

USA TODAY BESTSELLING AUTHOR

CARIDAD PIÑEIRO

Soldier's Secret Child

Silhouette®
Romantic
SUSPENSE

Special thanks and acknowledgment to
Caridad Piñeiro for her contribution to
The Coltons: Family First miniseries.

SILHOUETTE BOOKS

Recycling programs
for this product may
not exist in your area.

ISBN-13: 978-0-373-27610-3
ISBN-10: 0-373-27610-9

SOLDIER'S SECRET CHILD

Visit Silhouette Books at www.eHarlequin.com

Printed in U.S.A.

Books by Caridad Piñeiro

Silhouette Romantic Suspense

*Darkness Calls #1283
*Danger Calls #1371
*Temptation Calls #1390
Secret Agent Reunion #1476
More than a Mission #1498
Soldier's Secret Child #1540

Silhouette Nocturne

*Death Calls
*Devotion Calls
*Blood Calls
**Fate Calls

*The Calling
**Holiday with a Vampire

CARIDAD PIÑEIRO

is a *USA TODAY* and *New York Times* bestselling author of twenty novels. In 2007, a year marked by six releases from Harlequin Books and Pocket Books, Caridad was selected as the 2007 Golden Apple Author of the Year by the New York City Romance Writers. Caridad's novels have been lauded as the Best Short Contemporary Romance of 2001 in the NJ Romance Writers Golden Leaf Contest, Top Fantasy Books of 2005 and 2006 by *CATALINA* magazine and Top Nocturne of 2006 by *Cataromance*. Caridad has appeared on various television shows, such as the FOX News Early Edition in New York, and articles featuring her novels have been published in several leading newspapers and magazines, such as the *New York Daily News, Latina* and the *Star Ledger*. For more information on Caridad, please visit www.caridad.com or www.thecallingvampirenovels.com.

This book is dedicated to the men and women of the military and their families, without whom we could not have the liberties that make our daily lives possible.

Chapter 1

Macy Ward had never imagined that on her wedding day she would be running out of the church instead of walking down the aisle.

But just over a week earlier, she had been drawn out of the church by the sharp crack of gunshots and the harsh squeal of tires followed by the familiar sound of her fiancé's voice shouting for someone to get his police cruiser.

Her fiancé, Jericho Yates, the town sheriff and her lifelong friend. Her best friend in all the world and the totally wrong man to marry, she thought again, her hands tightening on the steering wheel. She shot a glance at her teenage son who sat beside her in the passenger seat.

"You ready for this, T.J.?"

He pulled out one earbud of his iPod. Tinny, too loud music blared from it. "Did you want something?" T.J. asked.

It was impossible to miss the sullen tones of his voice or the angry set of his jaw.

She had seen a similar irritated expression on the face of T.J.'s biological father, Fisher Yates, as he stood in his Army dress uniform outside the church with his brother—her fiancé. Fisher had looked far more attractive than he should have. As she had raced out into the midst of the bedlam occurring on the steps of the chapel, her gaze had connected with Fisher's stony glare for just a few seconds.

A few seconds too long.

When she had urged Jericho to go handle the incident and that they could postpone the wedding, she had seen the change in Fisher's gaze.

She wasn't sure if it had been relief at first. But the emotion that followed and lingered far longer had been more dangerous.

Now, there was no relief in T.J.'s hard glare. Just anger.

"Are you ready for this?" she repeated calmly, shooting him a glance from the corner of her eye as she drove to the center of town.

The loose black T-shirt T.J. wore barely shifted with his indifferent shrug. "Do I have any choice?"

Choice? Did anyone really have many choices in life? she thought, recalling how she would have chosen not to get pregnant by Fisher. Or lose her husband, Tim, to cancer. Or have a loving and respectful son turn into a troublesome seventeen-year-old hellion.

"You most certainly have choices, T.J. You could have failed your math class or gone to those tutoring sessions. You could have done time in juvie instead of community service. And now—"

"I'll have to stay out of trouble by working at the ranch since you decided not to marry Jericho."

It had been Jericho who had persuaded a judge to spare T.J. a juvenile record. The incident in question had resulted in rolls and rolls of toilet paper all over an old teacher's prized landscaped lawn and a mangled mailbox that had needed to be replaced.

"After postponing the wedding, I realized that I was getting married for all the wrong reasons. So, I chose not to go ahead with the wedding and I'm glad that I did. It gave Jericho the chance to find someone he truly loves," she said, clasping and unclasping her hands on the wheel as she pulled into a spot in front of the post office.

"I told you before that I don't need another dad," he said, but his words were followed by another shrug as T.J.'s head dropped down. "Not that Jericho isn't a nice guy. He's just not my dad."

Macy killed the engine, cradled her son's chin and applied gentle pressure to urge his head upward. "I know you miss him. I do, too. It's been six long years without him, but he wouldn't want you to still be unhappy."

"And you think working at the ranch with some gnarly surfer dude from California will make me happy?" He jerked away from her touch and wagged one hand in the familiar hang loose surfer sign.

She dropped her hands into her lap and shook her head, biting back tears and her own anger. As a recreational therapist, she understood the kinds of emotions T.J. was venting with his aggressive behavior. Knew how to try to get him to open up about his feelings.

But as a mother, the attitude was frustrating.

"Jewel tells me Joe is a great kid and he's your age. Maybe you'll find that you have something in common."

Without waiting for his reply, she grabbed her purse and rushed out of the car, crossed the street and made a beeline for the door to Miss Sue's. She had promised her boss, Jewel Mayfair, that she would stop by the restaurant to pick up some of its famous sticky buns for the kids currently residing at the Hopechest Ranch.

When she reached the door, however, she realized *he* was there.

Fisher Yates.

Decorated soldier, Jericho's older brother and unknown to him or anyone else in town, T.J.'s biological father. Only her husband, Tim, had known, and he had kept the secret to his grave.

The morning that had started out so-so due to T.J.'s moodiness just went to bad. She would have no choice but to acknowledge Fisher on her way to the take-out counter in the back of the restaurant. Especially since he looked up and noticed her standing there. His green-eyed gaze narrowed as he did so and his full lips tightened into a grim line.

He really should loosen up and smile some more, she thought, recalling the Fisher of her youth who had always had a grin ready for her, Tim and Jericho.

Although she couldn't blame him for his seeming reticence around her. She had done her best to avoid him during the entire time leading up to the wedding. Had somehow handled being around him during all the last-minute preparations, being polite but indifferent whenever he was around. It was the only way to protect herself against the emotions which lingered about Fisher.

In the week or so since she and Jericho had parted ways, it had been easier since she hadn't seen Fisher around town and knew it was just a matter of time before he was back on duty and her secret would be safe again.

She ignored the niggle of guilt that Fisher didn't know about T.J. Or that as a soldier, he risked his life with each mission and might not ever know that he had a son. Over the years she had told herself it had been the right decision to make not just for herself, but for Fisher as well. Jericho had told her more than once over the years how happy his older brother was in the Army. How it had been the perfect choice for him.

As much as the guilt weighed heavily on her at times, she could not risk any more problems with her son by revealing such a truth now. T.J. had experienced enough upset lately and he was the single most important thing in her life. She would do anything to protect him. To see him smile once again.

Which included staying away from Fisher Yates no matter how much she wanted to make things right between them.

Fisher was just finishing up a plate of Miss Sue's famous buckwheat pancakes when he looked up and glimpsed Macy Ward at the door to the café.

She seemed to hesitate for a moment when she spied him and he wondered why.

Did she feel guilty about avoiding him the whole time he'd been home or was her contriteness all about her change of mind at the altar where she had left his brother? Not that it had been the wrong thing to do. From the moment his kid brother Jericho had told him about his decision to marry Macy, Fisher had believed it was a mistake.

Not that he was any kind of expert on marriage, having avoided it throughout his thirty-seven years of life, but it struck him as wrong to be in a loveless marriage. Jericho should have known that given the experience of his own parents.

Their alcoholic mother had walked out on the Yates men when he was nine and old enough to realize that if there had been any love between his mother and father, drink had driven it away a long time before.

Macy finally pushed through the door and as she passed him, she dipped her head in greeting and said, "Mornin'."

"Mornin'," he replied, and glanced surreptitiously at her as she passed.

At thirty-five years of age, Macy Ward was a fine-looking woman. Trim but with curves in all the right places.

Fisher remembered those curves well. Remembered the strength and tenderness in her toned arms and legs as she had held him. Remembered the passion of their one night which was just another reason why he had known it was wrong for his brother and Macy to marry.

He couldn't imagine being married to a woman like Macy and having the relationship be platonic. Hell, if it were him, he'd have her in bed at every conceivable moment.

Well, at every moment that he could given the presence of her seventeen-year-old son T.J.

Which made him wonder where the boy was until he peered through the windows of Miss Sue's and spotted him sitting in Macy's car. His mop of nearly-black hair, much darker than Macy's light brown, hung down in front of his face, obscuring anything above his tight-lipped mouth.

Fisher wondered if T.J. was angry about the aborted wedding. To hear Jericho talk, the teenager had been none too happy with the announcement, but to hear his father talk, there wasn't much that T.J. had been happy with since T.J.'s father's death from cancer six years earlier.

Not that he blamed the boy. It had taken him a long time to get over his own mother's abandonment. Some might say he never had given his wandering life as a soldier and his inability to commit to any woman.

From behind him he heard the soft scuff of boots across the gleaming tile floor and almost instinctively knew it was Macy on her way back. Funny in how only just a couple of weeks he could identify her step and the smell of her.

She always smelled like roses.

But then again, observing such things was a necessary part of his military training. An essential skill for keeping his men alive.

His men, he thought and picked up the mug of steaming coffee, sweet with fresh cream from one of the small local ranches. In a couple of weeks, he would either be heading back for another tour of duty in the Middle East or accepting an assignment back in the States as an instructor at West Point.

Although he understood the prestige of being assigned to the military academy, he wasn't sure he was up for settling down in one place.

Since the day eighteen years ago when Macy had walked down the aisle with Tim, he had become a traveling man and he liked it that way. No ties or connections other than to his dad, younger brother and his men. People he could count on, he thought as the door closed on Macy's firm butt encased in soft faded denim.

A butt his hands itched to touch along with assorted other parts of her.

With a mumbled curse, he took a sip of the coffee, wincing at its heat. Reminded himself that he was only in town for a short period of time.

Too little time to waste wondering over someone who probably hadn't given him a second thought in nearly twenty years.

Chapter 2

What made the drive to the Hopechest Ranch better wasn't just that it was shorter, Macy thought.

She loved the look of the open countryside and how it grew even more empty the farther they got away from Esperanza. The exact opposite of how it had been in the many years that she had made the drive to the San Antonio hospital where she had once worked.

Out here in the rugged Texas countryside, she experienced a sense of balance and homecoming. When Jewel Mayfair and the California side of the Colton family had bought the acres adjacent to the Bar None in order to open the Hopechest Ranch, Macy had decided she had wanted to work there. Luckily, she and Jewel had hit it off during her interview.

It wasn't just that they had similar ideas about dealing with the children at the ranch or that tragedy had touched both their lives. They were both no-nonsense rational women with a strong sense of family, honor and responsibility.

They had bonded immediately and their friendship had grown over the months of working together, so much so that she had asked Jewel to be her maid of honor.

Because she was a friend and understood her all too well, Jewel hadn't pressed her since the day she had canceled the wedding, aware of Macy's concerns about marrying Jericho and her turmoil over the actions of her son.

Macy was grateful for that as well as Jewel's offer to hire T.J. to work during the summer months at the ranch.

At seventeen, he was too old for after school programs, not to mention that for the many years she had worked in San Antonio, she had felt guilty about having him in such programs. Before Tim's death, T.J. used to go home and spend time with his father, who had been a teacher at one of the local schools.

She pulled up in front of the Spanish-style ranch house, which was the main building at the Hopechest Ranch. The Coltons had spared no expense in building the sprawling ranch house that rose up out of the flat Texas plains. Attention to detail was evident in every element of the house from the carefully maintained landscaping to the ornate hand-carved wooden double doors at the entrance.

Macy was well aware, however, that the Hopechest Ranch wasn't special because of the money the Coltons lavished on the house and grounds. It was the love the Coltons put into what they did with the kids within. She mumbled a small prayer that the summer spent here might help her work a change in T.J.'s attitude.

She parked off to one side of the driveway, shut off the engine and they both stepped out of the car.

One of the dark wooden doors opened immediately.

Ana Morales stepped outside beneath the covered portico by the doors, her rounded belly seeming even larger today than it had the day before. The beautiful young Mexican woman laid a hand on one of the columns of the portico as she waited for them.

Ana had taken refuge at the Hopechest Ranch like many of the others within, although the main thrust of the program at the ranch involved working with troubled children. Despite that, the young woman had been a welcome addition, possessing infinite patience with the younger children.

Sticky bun box in hand, Macy smiled and embraced Ana when she reached the door. "How are you today, *amiga?*"

"Just fine, Macy," Ana said, her expressive brown eyes welcoming. She shot a look over Macy's shoulder at T.J. "This is your son, no?"

She gestured to him. "T.J., meet Ms. Morales."

"Ana, *por favor,*" she quickly corrected. "He's very handsome and strong."

"Miss Ana," T.J. said, removing his hat and ducking his head down in embarrassment.

As they stepped within the foyer of the ranch, the noises of activity filtered in from the great rooms near the back of the ranch house and drew them to the large family room/-kitchen area. In the bright open space, half a dozen children of various ages and ethnicities moved back and forth between the kitchen, where Jewel and one of the Hopechest Ranch's housekeepers were busy serving up family-style platters of breakfast offerings.

Ana immediately went to their assistance as did Macy, walking to the counter and grabbing a large plate for the sticky buns. Motioning with her head, she said, "Go grab yourself a spot at the table, T.J."

As the children noted that the food was being put out, they shifted to the large table between the family room and kitchen and soon only a few spots were free at the table.

T.J. hovered nervously beyond, uncertain.

Macy was about to urge her son to sit again when a handsome young man entered the room—Joe, she assumed. He had just arrived at the ranch and she hadn't had a chance to meet him yet.

Almost as tall as T.J., he had the same lanky build, but his hair was a shade darker. His hair was stylishly cut short around his ears, but longer up top framing bright blue eyes that inquisitively shifted over the many occupants of the room.

He walked over to stand beside T.J. and nodded his head, earning a return bop of his head from T.J.

"I'm Joe," he said and held out his hand.

"Just call me T.J.," her son answered and shook the other teen's hand.

"Looks good," Joe said and gestured to the food on the table. "Dude, I'm hungry. How about you?"

The loud growl from T.J.'s stomach was all the answer needed and Joe nudged him with his shoulder. "Come on, T.J. If you wait too long, the rugrats will get all the good stuff."

A small smile actually cracked T.J.'s lips before he followed Joe to the table. He hesitated again for a moment as Joe sat, leaving just one empty chair beside a dark-haired teen girl.

The teen, Sara Engelheit, a pretty sixteen-year-old who had come to the ranch recently, looked up shyly at T.J., who mumbled something beneath his breath, but then took the seat.

Macy released the breath she had been holding all that

time and as her gaze connected with Jewel's she noted the calm look on her boss's face. With a quick incline of her head, it was as if Jewel was saying, "I told you not to worry."

Jewel walked to the kids' table, excused herself and snagged one of the sticky buns, earning a raucous round of warnings from the children about eating something healthy.

Grinning, Jewel said, "I promise I'll go get some fresh juice and fruit."

Heeding the admonishments of the children, she, Ana and the housekeeper helped themselves to the eggs, oatmeal and other more nutritious offerings and then joined Jewel at a small café bar at one side of the great space, a routine they did every day.

Some of the children had rebelled at the routine at first, but they soon fell into the security of the routine. Happiness filled her as she noticed the easy camaraderie of the children around the table.

While they ate, the women discussed the day's schedule, reviewing what each of them would do as they split the children into age- and need-defined groups before reuniting them all during the day for meals.

When they were done, they turned their attention to their charges. Ana took the younger children to play at the swing set beyond the pool so they could avoid the later heat of the Texas summer day. Macy took the tweens and teens out to the corrals that housed an assortment of small livestock and some chickens. They loved the animals and learning to care for them helped her reinforce patterns of responsibility and teamwork.

As the groups were established, Jewel faced T.J. and Joe who were the eldest of the children present. "I'm going to ask the two of you to go with me today. You're both new to the ranch and I'd like to show you around. Give you an idea of the chores I expect you to do."

The boys stood side by side, nodded almost in unison, but as Jewel turned away for a moment, Macy noted the look that passed between them as if to say, "What have we gotten ourselves into?"

In that moment, she knew a bond had been established and only hoped that it would be one for the better given Jewel's accolades about Joe.

"Hurry up, Mom. I promised Joe I'd get there early so I can show him those XBOX cheat codes before breakfast," T.J. said and raced out of their house. The door slammed noisily behind him and normally she would have cautioned him about being more careful, but she didn't have the heart to do it. He seemed so eager to get to the ranch.

Rushing, she hopped on one booted foot, trying to step into the other boot while slipping on her jacket at the same time. Nearly pitching backward onto her ass, she grappled for the deacon's bench by the front door and chuckled at her own foolishness.

She was just so excited to finally see her son starting to lose some of his surliness. He actually looked forward to something.

She finished dressing with less haste and minutes later, they were on their way to the ranch, T.J. sitting beside her with his iPod running. Unlike his slouched stance of a week ago, he almost leaned forward, as if to urge them to move more quickly toward the ranch.

The countryside flashed beside them as they left the edge of town, the wide open meadows filled with the whites of wild plums, the maroon and yellow of Mexican hat and mountain pink wildflowers. Ahead of them a cloudless sky the color of Texas bluebonnets seemed to go on forever.

In less than ten minutes they were at Hopechest and she had barely stopped the car when T.J. went flying up the driveway and into the house. She proceeded more slowly, stopping to inhale the fresh scent of fresh cut summer grass and the flowers from a nearby meadow.

It was going to be a good day, she thought.

Inside the house, T.J., Joe and Sara were gathered around the XBOX in the family room, where as promised, T.J. was teaching them the cheat codes.

As the women did every day, they set up breakfast, ate and after they finished, Jewel announced to the kids that they had a special treat for them that day—Clay Colton was bringing over a mare to keep at the ranch for them to ride and care for.

T.J. and Joe had been at work all week in anticipation of the mare's arrival. They had cleaned up some of the stalls in one of the smaller barns on the property, placing fresh-smelling hay in one stall and setting up the other one to hold tack, feed and other necessities.

As the ragtag group walked to a corral on the property, the younger children were in front of the pack, followed by T.J., Joe and Sara.

Macy, Jewel and Ana took up spots at the side of the group, keeping an eye on the youngest as they approached the corral. Clay Colton waited astride his large roan stallion Crockett. A smaller palomino mare stood beside him and his horse.

Clay was all cowboy, she thought, admiring his easy seat on the saddle and the facility with which he swung off the immense mount. He ground tethered Crockett and then walked the mare over toward them.

"Mornin'," he said and tipped his white Stetson. Longish black hair peeked from beneath the hat and his eyes were a vivid blue against the deep tan of his skin.

"Mornin', Clay. We can't thank you enough for bringing the mare for the children," Jewel said.

"My pleasure. How about I show Joe and T.J. how to handle her for the younger kids?"

"That would be great, Clay. It'll be a big relief for both Jewel and me if the boys can control her. What's her name?" Macy asked.

Clay pushed his hat back a bit, exposing more of his face as he waved the two boys over. "Gentlemen, come on over and meet Papa's Poppy."

T.J. and Joe scrambled up and over the split rail corral fence, stood by Clay as he took the saddle, blanket, bit and reins off the mare. The horse stood by calmly as he did so and then later as Clay showed the boys how to place all the equipment back on.

T.J. already had a fairly good knowledge of what to do since he and his dad used to ride together. He seemed hesitant at first, but then Clay said, "That's the way, T.J. Good job."

His uncertainty seemed to fade then and before long, he and Joe had ridden the mare around the corral a time or two. The younger children were calling out eagerly to have a turn as well.

Joe slipped off the horse and handed the reins to T.J.

"Me? What am I supposed to do now?"

Clay clapped him on the back. "Keep her under control while Joe gets one of your friends up on her. She's gentle. You can handle it."

T.J. took a big gulp, but did as Clay asked and before long, the two boys were giving the remaining children their turns on the mare, Clay hovering nearby protectively until it was clear that T.J. and Joe were in charge of the situation.

He stepped over to where she stood with Jewel and Ana and said, "This will work out well for you, I think. Papa's Poppy is the gentlest mare I have."

"I insist on paying for her, Clay," Jewel said, facing him.

Clay shrugged and the fabric of his western shirt stretched tight against shoulders made broad by years of ranch work. "She was an injured stray I found a year or so ago. All scratched up from a fight with some prickly poppy she got tangled up in."

"Hence the name," she said.

"Yep and to be honest, you'd be helping me out by taking her. I need room for a new stud I want to buy for the Bar None."

"Are there many strays in the area, Clay?" Jewel asked as she leaned on the top rail of the fence, vigilantly keeping an eye on the children.

"Occasionally. Why do you ask?" he said and pulled off his hat, wiped at a line of sweat with a bandanna.

Jewel dragged a hand through the short strands of her light brown hair, suddenly uneasy. "I've heard noises in the night."

"Me, too," Ana chimed in. "It sounds like a baby crying or maybe a small animal in pain."

"Yes, exactly," Jewel confirmed. "Not all the time, just every now and then."

Clay jammed his white Stetson back on his head and glanced in the direction of the two boys, squinting against the sun as he did so. "I haven't heard anything up my way, but I can swing by one night and check it out for you."

He motioned with a work-roughened hand to the two boys. "They'll make fine ranch hands. Remind me of Ryder and myself when we were kids. We loved being around the horses more than anything."

Macy couldn't miss the wistfulness in his voice as Clay spoke of his younger brother. Much like T.J., Ryder had begun getting into trouble as a teen, but then it had gotten progressively worse until Ryder had ended up in jail for smuggling aliens across the border.

"Have you heard from your brother lately?" she asked, wondering if Clay had relented from his stance to disavow his troubled brother.

"I wrote to him, but the mail came back as undeliverable." A hard set entered his jaw and his bright blue eyes lost the happy gleam from watching the children.

"Maybe your brother was moved?" Ana offered, laying a gentle hand on Clay's arm.

He nodded and smiled stiffly. "Maybe, Miss Ana. I just hope it's not too late to make amends with my little brother. I'm going to try to call someone at the prison to see what's happening with him."

"I think you're right to put the past behind you and try to make things right with Ryder," Jewel added, but then stepped away to help the boys with one of the younger children who seemed to be afraid of the mare.

Ana went over as well to help since the child was Mexican and still learning English, leaving Macy alone with Clay.

"You'll work things out with your brother," she said, trying to offer comfort. Clay was a good man and she hated to see him upset.

"I hope so. It's never too late to make amends with the people from our past, Macy. You should understand that more than some," he said, surprising her.

She examined his face, searching for the meaning behind his words. Wondering if he somehow knew about her and Fisher. About T.J.

"I do understand," she said, waiting for him to say more so that she could confirm the worst of her fears, but he didn't. Instead, he shouted out his farewell to everyone, walked over to his stallion and climbed up into his saddle.

"Take good care of her, men. I'll be back later to show you how to groom her, handle the feeding and keep the stall clean," he added with a wave to the boys before leaving.

Both T.J. and Joe straightened higher at his comment. She hadn't been wrong in wanting to marry Jericho to give her son a man's presence in his life. It was obvious from just this slight interaction that both boys had responded positively to the added responsibility and to being treated as adults.

Small steps. Positive ones.

She should be grateful for that, but Clay's words rang in her head as she stepped over to help Jewel and Ana with the rest of the children.

It's never too late to make amends with the people from our past.

As much as she hoped that he was right, she also prayed that she would not have to make amends before T.J. was ready to handle it.

Chapter 3

The mare had been a wonderful addition to their program at the ranch, Macy thought as she watched the teens working together in the stalls and adjacent corral.

She and Jewel had discussed how to incorporate the responsibilities for the mare into a program for the children. They had broken them up into rotating teams that took turns with the mare's care and feeding. In addition, she worked with the tweens and teens, including T.J. and Joe, to improve how they handled the mare. Setting up a series of small tests, she encouraged each of the teens until they were all able to take turns not only outfitting and riding the mare, but watching and helping the younger children with the horse.

When T.J. and Joe weren't with the groups, they were off finishing up some of the other chores around the ranch, including a ride with Clay Colton to attempt to track down the elusive sounds that Jewel was still hearing at night. But they returned from that expedition with little to show for it.

She was grateful that T.J. and Joe seemed to have bonded so quickly and so well. As the eldest amongst the children at the ranch, the others seemed to look up to them, in particular the tweens and Sara, the petite young teen who had recently joined them.

It wasn't unusual to see the three of them together at meals and as they took an afternoon break at the pool during the heat of the day, much as they were doing today.

As she watched them frolicking in the cool waters, Jewel stepped up beside her.

"Things seem to be better," her friend said.

"I had hopes for it, but this is more than I expected so quickly."

"Let's take a break." Jewel gestured to a small table located on the covered courtyard where someone had placed a pitcher with iced tea and glasses. A few feet away from the table in the middle of the courtyard was a fountain. The sounds of the running water combined with the scents from the riot of flowers surrounding the courtyard were always calming.

With a quick nod, she sat at the table and poured tea into the two glasses, all the time keeping an eye on what was going on in the pool.

T.J. and Joe led the younger children in a game of Marco Polo, while Sara sat by the side, arms wrapped around herself in a slightly defensive stance.

"We've still got to get Sara to open up a bit," she said.

Jewel picked up her glass and took a sip. "She's been better since the boys got here, but she hasn't been willing to say much during our one-on-one sessions."

"Nothing about the bruises or why she ran away?" she asked, thinking of the purpling marks and fingerprints that had been on the girl's arms on the day she had arrived at the ranch a few weeks ago.

"Nothing and you know our rule."

"We wait until our charge is ready to talk. Do you have another session scheduled with her anytime soon?" She sipped her tea, sighed as the cool liquid slid down her heat parched throat. She hadn't realized just how hot and dry it had been as she and the teens had worked with the mare all morning.

"I have a group session with the older children this afternoon. I was thinking to ask T.J. and Joe to join us."

She thought of T.J.'s anger at his dad's passing and of Joe's adoption by the Coltons. Certainly both of the boys had things to unload and considering how well the group had been getting along, it seemed like a good idea.

"Both T.J. and Joe might have things they want to talk about. I'd ask to sit in, but I know T.J. might be more willing to open up if I'm not around."

Jewel laid a hand on hers as it rested on the table, shifting her iced tea back and forth in the condensation from the glass. "I know that hurts, but you're right. T.J. will likely be more open if you're not around. But I'll keep you posted about what happens. This way you'll know how to deal with it."

Macy took hold of Jewel's hand and gave it a reassuring squeeze. "Thanks. I'd appreciate anything you can say without violating doctor/patient confidentiality."

"Deal," she confirmed and then they sat back and took a moment just to enjoy the peacefulness of the midday break.

* * *

Macy was working with two of the younger children when she noticed the teens walking out of the living room where Jewel often held the group therapy sessions.

The two tween boys had their arms around each other's shoulders and their heads together, talking.

T.J., Joe and Sara followed behind closely, but then split away, walking through the great space and then out to the pool area. They kept on walking beyond the tract of grass with the swing set and Macy assumed T.J. and Joe were off to do the last of their afternoon chores.

Once in the great room, the tween boys headed immediately to the XBOX and she could hear them carrying on about the tricks Joe and T.J. had taught them.

She smiled at the worship of the older boys, but her smile faded as she noted Jewel's face. Excusing herself from the memory game, but urging the children to continue on their own, she approached her boss.

"You look wiped."

"Mark finally opened up today. Told the other kids about how his dad used to beat him."

Both of them suspected that Mark had been physically abused from his manner when he had first come to the ranch, but having him admit it was a good step to helping him deal with the trauma.

"How about Sara?" she wondered, thinking that maybe Mark's revelation would have encouraged the young girl to tell her own story.

Jewel shook her head. "Nothing. She just sat there, arms wrapped around herself. Silent."

"Sorry to hear that, but she is coming out of her shell. She seems to talk to T.J. and Joe a lot."

"That's a good start. Where are they?" Jewel asked as she scanned the great room and saw no sign of them.

"I saw them heading out back, probably to finish up their chores before the weekend. I'll go see what they're up to," she said and at her boss's cue of approval, she went in search of them.

As she suspected, they were at the corral, but not working. The two boys sat on the top rail of the fence, Sara between them, head bowed down.

She was about to approach to make sure everything was okay, but then T.J. brought his hand up and patted Sara's back in a familiar gesture. She had seen Tim do it more than once when comforting his young son and it twisted her heartstrings that Tim would not see the man T.J. would become.

Which was followed by a wave of guilt as she realized that maybe Fisher never would either if she didn't tell him about his son. If she didn't make amends for what had happened in the past between them.

Certain that the teens were better off without her presence at that moment, she returned to the ranch house and the game of memory she had left earlier.

But even then she experienced no relief as the children matched up the first few letters.

F.

S.

I.

Certainly someone somewhere was telling her it was time to consider what she would do about Fisher.

Fisher sat across from his dad in Miss Sue's, enjoying the last of his ribs and delicious fries.

It wasn't as if he and his dad couldn't have made themselves dinner. Since their mom had left, the three men had learned how to provide for themselves, but with it being Friday night and all, they needed a treat.

Plus, he hadn't wanted to waste time cooking when he could be spending it talking to his dad, especially since his time in Esperanza was ticking away quickly. Just a few more weeks and he would head back to the military.

As he ran a fry through the ketchup and ate the last piece of tender meat on the rib, the cowbell clanged over the door. A trio walked in—Macy's son with another boy and a teen girl.

They stopped at the door to wait to be seated. As the hostess showed them to a booth, they passed by.

"Evening, Mr. Yates," T.J. said to his dad and nodded at Fisher in greeting as well.

"Evening, T.J. Are these friends of yours?" Buck Yates asked, flicking his large hand in the direction of the other teens with T.J.

"Yes, sir, they are. Joe and Sara, meet Mr. Yates. He's the sheriff's dad and this is the sheriff's brother—Captain Yates."

Joe and Sara shook hands with the men and then the trio excused themselves.

"Polite young man," Fisher said, slightly surprised given the accounts provided by his brother about T.J.'s antics.

"He's a good kid, just a little angry ever since his pa died," Buck said and pushed away his empty plate.

"It must have been rough," he said, imagining how difficult it would have been on both Macy and T.J. His own brother had suffered greatly as well since Tim had been his lifelong best friend.

Luckily, Jericho had been Macy's best friend also and had

been by her side during the long months that Tim had battled cancer. At least Macy hadn't been alone, but it didn't stop the sudden clenching of his gut that maybe he could have been there for her, as well.

He drove that thought away quickly. Being away from Macy was up there on the list of reasons he had joined the military.

Maybe the top reason, he mused, thinking back to the night that had forever sealed the course of his life.

Chapter 4

Esperanza, Texas
Eighteen years earlier

Jericho stood at the plate, bat held high. His hips shifting back and forth, his body relaxed. He waited for the pitch.

Jericho's team was down by one. Tim Ward was on third base and another player on second with two men out. It would be the last inning unless they were able to get some runs on the board.

Fisher sat beside his dad on the bleacher and called out encouragement. "You can do it, Jericho."

His yell was followed by Macy's from where she sat a few feet away and a row down from them. "Go-o-o, Jericho-o. One little hit."

She sat beside Jericho's latest girlfriend. He couldn't remember her name because Jericho never kept a girl for too long, much like him. The Yates boys were love 'em and leave 'em kinds of guys, he thought.

Macy, on the other hand, wasn't a love 'em and leave 'em type of girl. Until recently, everyone thought she and Tim were a forever kind of thing what with them going off to college together. Except that in the past few weeks, Macy and Tim didn't seem to be a thing anymore, which meant that Tim had loved her and left her. That struck him as downright stupid.

The crack of the bat pulled his attention away from thoughts of Macy.

Jericho had lined a rocket of a hit up the first baseline and deep into the corner of the stadium. Tim would score easily to tie the game, but as people got up on the bleachers and started cheering, it was clear the ball was deep enough to maybe score the man from second.

The outfielder picked up the ball and with all his might sent it flying home, but the man from second was already well on his way to the plate. The ball sailed past the catcher as the man slid into home to win the game.

The wild cheering and revelry of the hometown crowd spurred on the players who ran out onto the field to celebrate the victory. After a few moments of exuberant celebration, both the players and the crowd finally quieted down and the players formed a line to shake hands with the other team.

As they did so, the crowd began to disperse from the stands.

"I'll see you at home, son," his dad said, clapped him on the back and waved at Jericho on the field.

He jumped down from the bleachers and weaved through the crowd of well-wishers until he reached Jericho, whose new girlfriend was already plastered to his hip.

Tim and Macy stood across from one another awkwardly, clearly no longer a forever kind of thing and surprisingly, he was kind of glad about that.

"Hey, big bro," Jericho said as he joined them. "Tim, Cindy and I are heading to Bill's for a post-baseball bash. Want to come hang with us?"

All three of them, but not Macy? he wondered and shot a glance at her as she stood there, hands laced primly together in front of her.

"No thanks, lil' bro. Just came down to say congrats on winning the game."

"We've gotta run. What about you, Mace?" Jericho said, either clearly oblivious to the tension between his two friends or choosing to ignore it.

"I've got…things to do," she replied, peeking up at him from the corner of her eye.

"We're history, then," Jericho said and left with Cindy bumping hips with him on one side and Tim on the other.

He jammed the tips of his fingers into the pockets of his jeans and rocked back on the heels of his boots, hesitant now that he and Macy were alone. "So what's so important for you to have to do on a Friday night?"

A blast of pink brightened her cheeks before she straightened her shoulders and faced him head on, determination in her brown-eyed gaze. "Well, since it's early, I was thinking of maybe grabbing a bite at Miss Sue's. Are you hungry?" After she asked, she worried her bottom lip with her teeth, belying her nervousness around him.

He was hungry, but not necessarily for anything other than a taste of that luscious bottom lip. Years earlier he'd had a taste during what was supposed to be a chaste holiday kiss, but he had underestimated the potency of her kiss. That encounter had made him realize that like Tim, he had been smitten by tomboy Macy Ward.

"I'm hungry, but won't Tim mind, you know…you and me. Friday night. Dinner."

She cocked her head at him defiantly. "What I do is no longer any of Tim's concern. So, dinner?"

Interesting, he thought, but quickly offered her his arm. "Dinner it is. My treat."

He wanted to lick the plate of the last remnants of Miss Sue's famous apple cobbler, but his dad had raised him to be a gentleman so he held back.

Macy must have seen the hunger that remained in his gaze since she offered up the last few bites of the pie on her plate. "You can finish mine."

His mouth watered at the site of those extra pieces, but he shook his head. "I couldn't take the last of your dessert."

"Go ahead. I need to watch my figure anyway," she said, moving aside his plate and pushing hers before him.

Fisher dug into the cobbler, but after he swallowed a bite, he said, "Seems to me you're worrying for nothing, Mace."

Truth be told, she had a wonderful figure. Trim and strong, but with womanly curves in all the right places. As he thought about that, he shifted in his seat as his jeans tightened painfully. He had imagined those curves next to him once too often since that fateful kiss.

"Something wrong, Fisher?" she asked, innocently unaware of the effect she had on him.

"Not at all," he lied, quickly finished the cobbler and paid the tab.

With his hand on the small of her back, he walked her out to the sidewalk where they stood there for a moment, enjoying the early summer night. Dusk was just settling in, bringing with it the cooler night air and the soft intimate glow of the streetlights along Main Street.

"Thank you for dinner," Macy said, glad for not only the fine food, but his company. He had always been a distant fourth musketeer to their little group and tonight she had been able to enjoy his presence without interference.

As he turned to look at her, she noticed the gleam in his green eyes. The kind of gleam that kicked her heart up into a hurried little beat. She might have been going out with Tim for as long as she could remember, but she could still recognize when a man found her attractive. And considering her breakup with Tim, it was a welcome balm that someone as attractive as Fisher appeared to be interested.

He smiled, his teeth white against his tanned skin and his dark five o'clock shadow. He was the kind of man who needed to shave more than twice a day. He was a man, she reminded herself, trying to ignore the pull of her attraction to him. Nothing like Jericho and Tim, even though Fisher was only two years older. There had always been a maturity and intensity about him that had set him apart from the others.

"It's early still," he said, the tones of his voice a soft murmur in the coming quiet of the night.

"It is," she said.

He leaned toward her and a lock of nearly jet-black hair fell forward onto his forehead as he said, "Too early to call it a night, don't you think?"

She met his gaze, glittering brightly with interest, the color like new spring grass. Kicking up that erratic beat of her heart and making her want to reach up and brush away that wild errant lock of hair.

"Did you have something in mind?" she asked in a breathless voice she didn't recognize.

"How about a drive? I'll even put the top down on the CJ."

She imagined driving through the night, Fisher beside her. The scents of the early summer wildflowers whipping around them as they sped along in the open Jeep through the Texas countryside.

"I think that sounds really nice."

They drove through the open meadows and fields surrounding Esperanza, the scented wind wrapping them in its embrace while bright moonlight lit the road before them until Fisher took a dirt road to one of the few nearby hills. He parked the CJ so it faced the lights of town and the wide starlit Texas sky.

She imagined she could see the lights of San Antonio, well to the south of their hometown. She and Tim had planned on going to college together there until Tim had said he was reconsidering that decision. She gazed at the lights of Esperanza and noticed the cars parked around Bill's house where Jericho and Tim would be with the rest of the baseball team. Where she might have been a few weeks earlier if things hadn't changed recently.

"Penny for your thoughts," he said and pushed back some strands of wind-blown hair from her face. The pads of his fingers brushed the sensitive skin of her cheek, sending a shiver rocketing through her body.

"Do you ever wonder if some things happen for a reason?" she asked.

"Meaning?" He arched one dark brow in question.

"Tim and me. His breaking it off." She shrugged and turned in her seat to face him. "If it hadn't been for that—"

"Being the nice girl that you are, you wouldn't be here tonight." He once again brushed the tips of his fingers across her cheek, then trailed them down to cup her jaw.

"Is that what you think I am? A nice girl?" she shot back, slightly perturbed, which was ridiculous. She was a nice girl, unlike many of the women with whom Fisher had been seen around town.

"Don't get so riled, Mace. There's nothing wrong with being a nice girl."

The words shot out of her mouth before she could censor them. "And boys like you don't think about doing things with nice girls."

"Boys like me?" he asked with another pointed arch of his brow and a wry smile on his lips.

Macy fidgeted with her hands, plucking at the seat belt she still wore. "You know, love 'em and leave 'em types like you."

He chuckled and shook his head, but he never broke the contact of his hand against her chin. Instead, he inched his thumb up to brush softly across her lips.

"Let's get something straight, Mace. First of all, I'm not a boy, I'm a man. A man whose daddy would tan his hide for the thoughts he's having right now about the nice girl who happens to be sitting next to him."

The warmth on the pad of his thumb spread itself across her lips and with his words, shot through the rest of her body. "Thoughts? What kinds of thoughts?"

He chuckled again, only with something darker and dangerously sexy this time. "You always were the daring type."

"He who dares, wins," she reminded him.

The smile on his face broadened and he leaned toward her until the warmth of his breath replaced that of his thumb against her lips. "Then I guess I should dare," he said and brought his lips to hers.

The shock of his hard mouth against hers was quickly replaced by a sense of...rightness which surprised her considering that this was Jericho's brother. That up until a few weeks ago, she had thought she was about to embark on a life with another man.

Another man who had rejected her. Who had never made her feel the way Fisher now made her feel.

The tip of his tongue tasted her lips, gently asked for entrance at the seam of her mouth. She opened her lips and accepted the thrust of his tongue. Joined it with hers until they were both breathing heavily and had to break apart for air.

Fisher turned away from her and clenched his hands on his thighs, struggling for control. This was Macy, he reminded himself, rubbing his hands across the soft denim of his jeans. Jericho's best friend and Tim's intended, he recalled as he held back from reaching for her again.

Only she wasn't Tim's anymore, the voice inside his head challenged and then urged, *And now she can be yours.*

He faced her and seeing the desire in her eyes, he asked, "Are you sure about this?"

She nodded quickly and he didn't second guess her decision. Reaching into the backseat of the CJ, he grabbed a blanket he kept there and stepped out of the car. Swinging around the front, he met her by the passenger side door and slipped his hand into hers. Twined his fingers with hers as he led her a few feet away from the Jeep to a soft spot of grass on the overlook.

He released her only long enough to spread out the blanket and then he urged her down.

For long moments they lay side by side on their backs, staring up at the late May moon. Listening to the rustle of the light breeze along the taller grass and the profusion of wild-flowers that perfumed the air.

Fisher rolled onto his side and ran the back of his index finger along the high straight ridge of her cheek. He had known her all his life and had thought she was the prettiest woman he had ever seen.

"You're beautiful."

Much like before, an embarrassed flush worked across her cheeks as she avoided his gaze. "I bet you say that to all the girls."

He laughed and shook his head. "Now why do you think I'm such a hound dog?"

"Because I've seen you around town with all those dangerous women," she answered and the blush along her cheeks deepened.

"Jealous?" he asked, but then immediately confessed, "Because every time I saw you with Tim, I was jealous."

A little jolt of excitement rattled her body before Macy turned onto her side and cradled his cheek. His five o'clock shadow tickled the palm of her hand. As she met his gaze, made a silvery green by the light of the moon, she detected no deception there, just honesty.

"Why didn't you—"

"You were Tim's girl and Jericho's best friend. I wasn't going to be responsible for breaking up the Three Muske-teers," he said and shrugged.

"And now?" she asked, mimicking his earlier move by

bringing her thumb to trace the warm fullness of his lips which broadened into a sexy dimpled smile with her caress.

"He who dares, wins," he said and brought his lips to hers.

Chapter 5

"I've never seen a smile like that one before," Buck Yates said as he signaled for the waitress, who immediately came over.

"I bet I know what you'd like, Buck," she said as she picked up the empty plates from the table. "A slice of Miss Sue's famous cherry pie and some coffee."

"You know me too well, Lizzy. How about you, Fisher? Was it something sweet that put that smile on your face?" Buck teased.

Something sweet and hot, Fisher thought, recalling the taste of Macy's lips and the warmth of her body pressed to his as they had made love that long ago night.

Shifting in his seat to readjust his increasingly tight jeans, he looked up at the perky young waitress. "I'll take a slice of that pie with some vanilla ice cream, please."

He needed the chill to cool down his thoughts.

As Lizzy walked away with their empty plates and orders, Buck once again resumed the earlier conversation. "So what had you smiling like the cat that ate the cream? A woman, and I hope a decent one at that."

With some force, Fisher shook his head. "Come on, Pa. You know I can't offer a decent woman the kind of life she'd want."

"Nonsense," Buck began and for emphasis, jabbed a gnarly index finger in his direction. "Plenty of military men have wives and families."

He couldn't argue with his dad, although he understood how difficult it was for such men. Being away from their families for months on end. The fears and dangers that each new mission brought for those left behind.

"I don't think I could share my kind of life with a woman."

His father was about to speak when Lizzy returned with the pies and coffee, but as soon as she left them, his dad continued his plea. "You could if you took that teaching assignment at West Point."

For weeks since the offer had come, he had been debating between that and returning for another tour of duty in the Middle East. As captain of his squad, he had recently led his men safely through three tours. He couldn't imagine leaving them.

"I don't want to abandon my men. Besides, I like the military life. It's orderly. Disciplined."

"Lonely," Buck jumped in. "At the end of the day when you hang up that uniform with all those medals—"

"I'll know that I helped bring home alive as many men as I could. Their families will thank me for that," he replied and forked up a bit of the pie and ice cream. The taste was wooden in his mouth because a part of him recognized that on some level his father was right.

At the end of his career, no matter how successful he had been, his uniform would hang in a closet empty of any traces of a woman or family. Despite that, he couldn't picture himself as a father or husband. Solving a family's problems instead of those of his men. He wasn't sure how to handle such things.

While glancing down at his pie, he said, "I know you'd like grandkids to carry on the Yates name, Pa. Seems to me Jericho's the one you should look to for that."

"Hard to believe it's only been a couple of weeks since he met Olivia and married her," his father said.

"I admire that Jericho's willing to claim Olivia's baby as his own and if I know my brother—"

"He'll be wanting more with her. I can see how much he cares for Olivia and it really makes me happy. I always worried after what happened with your ma—"

"Don't blame yourself. You did what you could and we all know we were better off without her," he said and yet a part of him acknowledged that her leaving had ripped away a piece of each of them. That for him and Jericho, it had made them leery of loving a woman for fear of being abandoned again.

Like Macy had abandoned him, he thought, recalling how despite their one night of incredible passion she had walked down the aisle with Tim Ward just over a month later.

His dad must have picked up on his upset. "You shouldn't let your ma leaving eat away at your gut like that. Neither you or Jericho had anything to do with that."

"You're right, Pa," he said, wanting to foreclose any further discussion. Wanting to forget anything and everything relating to Macy Ward.

He wasn't meant for women like her or for a family kind

of life. The military was what had brought order and happiness to his life eighteen years earlier.

It was what would bring order and happiness to his life for the future.

For the first Friday night in too many months, Macy felt like she could actually just kick back and relax.

The change in T.J. in a little over a week was a welcome surprise. He had clearly bonded not only with Joe, but with Sara. She hoped that friendship would help the young girl come out of her shell and talk about her problems. The Hopechest Ranch policy was not to press for details, but offer refuge. She knew, however, that she did the most good when the children were finally able to talk about their traumas.

Maybe Sara's friendship with T.J. and Joe would help her trust them enough to share and begin the road to healing.

Much as T.J. seemed to be healing.

In addition to the bonding, T.J. and Joe had completed each and every task that had been asked of them at the ranch and eagerly helped out with the other kids during their free time. Because of his exemplary behavior, when T.J. had asked if he could go to town with Joe and Sara, she had unequivocally said "Yes."

Which meant she had time to just unwind. Rare time in her normally hectic life.

She had filled her big claw-footed tub with steaming hot water and added some fragrant rose oils that Jewel had given her as an engagement gift. She had attempted to return them after she cancelled the wedding, but Jewel had insisted she keep them so she could treat herself.

Treat herself she would, she thought, tying the lush terry

cloth robe around herself and pouring a glass of wine to take with her to the bath. On the way, she snagged her brand-new romance novel from the nightstand in her bedroom.

Tim had always teased her about her romances until she had insisted he read them to her at night before bed.

He had never complained again after that, she thought with a smile as she set the book and wine on the painted wrought iron caddy. It perfectly matched the Victorian look of her bathroom, her one touch of fanciful in her otherwise modest and plain home.

She might have taken the Victorian theme further in the house, but realized it might have made it a little too girly for T.J. and had refrained from doing so. But in here and her bedroom—her private domain—she let herself give into her fantasies.

She slipped into the tub and the heat of the water immediately began to soak away some of the aches and tiredness. She loved working at the ranch, but with half a dozen children and the two teen boys, it was always a whirlwind of activities and quite physical.

The activities, however, were clearly making progress with some of the children. In the months she had been at the ranch, she had seen noticeable improvements not only in their academic skills, but their social ones. Kids who had once been loners were finally coming out of their shells.

It was what made her career so rewarding.

Grabbing the book off the caddy, she cracked it open and began to read, only she hadn't realized it was a book with a hero in the military. It normally didn't bother her, but her emotions were too unsettled with Fisher in town and so she set the book aside and picked up her wineglass.

As she took a sip, she recalled the sight of him and Jericho standing outside the church. Jericho had been so handsome in his tuxedo, but it had been Fisher standing there in his Army uniform, medals gleaming in the sun, that had caused her heart to skip a beat.

Even if she hadn't had any doubts about her marriage to Jericho before then, that reaction alone would have made her realize she was making a big mistake.

No matter how much she tried to forget it, her one and only night with Fisher had left an indelible memory. One she had driven deep inside her heart when she had made the decision to marry Tim Ward.

The right decision, she reminded herself as she took a small sip of the wine.

She and Tim had been destined to be together, their short breakup in high school notwithstanding. Tim was kind and patient and honorable. When she had told him she was pregnant just a short time before their wedding, he had been understanding and had even talked to her about telling Fisher.

She had considered it back then and in the many years since. But Jericho had been going on and on about how happy Fisher was in the Army and since their night together, Fisher never approached her again.

Talk had been that Fisher was the kind of man who couldn't commit and back then she felt he had loved and left her. When she had heard about his enlistment in the Army, it had made no sense to ruin his life by telling him about a child he probably wouldn't want.

But then she recalled the way he had looked at her on the steps of the church. Imagined she had seen desire in his gaze along with hurt. Not that she could hurt him unless he actually had feelings for her. Something which she didn't want to consider because it would complicate things.

Forcing her mind from such troubling thoughts, she placed her nearly untouched glass of wine on the caddy and sank farther into the bone-melting heat of the water. The fragrance of roses wafted around her, reminding her of the profusion of wild rose bushes tangled amongst the small stands of trees just outside the Esperanza town limits.

Reminding her of how the night had smelled while she made love with Fisher.

She shot upright in the bath, mumbling a curse, but then the phone rang and she mumbled yet another curse.

She had left the portable phone in her room.

As it continued to ring, demanding her attention, she climbed out of the bath, grabbed a towel and wrapped it around her. She raced to her bedroom to pick up before the answering machine kicked in.

Unfortunately, the answering machine engaged just as she reached it and heard across the speaker, "Mrs. Ward. This is Deputy Rawlings."

Her stomach dropped at the identity of the caller. At his next words, sadness and disappointment filled her soul. "I've got your son down at the station."

Chapter 6

T.J. walked out of the sheriff's office beside her, his body ramrod straight and stiff with tension. He hadn't offered up much of an explanation for the speeding which had led to his running into another car just on the outskirts of town.

Luckily the damage to both cars had been minor and no one had been injured. But because of their age and the speeding, the Deputy had decided to take the boys in and call her and Jewel.

She looked over her shoulder at her boss who walked beside Joe. The teen had a hangdog look on his face and clearly seemed to be sorry for what had happened.

Unlike T.J.

As they exited the police station, she spotted Fisher strolling out of Lone Star Square. Judging from the activity in the square, the movie had apparently just let out in the theater on the other side of the plaza. Some of the people headed to the cars parked all along the edges of the central space while Fisher and another couple waited to cross the street. He noticed them leaving the police station and condemnation flashed across his features.

It made her want to go over and wipe that critical look from his face, but she plowed forward. Speaking with T.J. about what had happened tonight needed to be her number one priority right now.

As they approached the parking lot, she inspected yet again the damage to T.J.'s car—a big ugly dent along the front bumper and part of the passenger side panel of the 1974 Pontiac GTO.

The GTO that his dad had bought as a rusty heap and had been restoring for years before his death. The GTO that T.J. had also been, as he called it, "pimping."

She paused before the car and stared at the damage before she looked up and met Jewel's concerned gaze, Joe's sheepish one and T.J.'s stony countenance.

"Luckily no one was hurt and the damage to both cars can be repaired. When we get home, we'll discuss how you're going to pay for those repairs and the speeding ticket," she said. Handing T.J. the keys to the GTO, she finished, "I'll follow you home."

Turning to Jewel, she noticed her friend's concern, but also Jewel's interest in Fisher as she glanced back across Main Street toward where he still stood on the edge of Lone Star Square, watching them.

She laid a hand on her friend's arm. "Can we talk about it in the morning? It's late and we should all be heading home."

Jewel nodded, faced Joe and said, "Let's go. You and I have a lot to discuss, as well."

As the two walked away, Macy waited for T.J. to get in his car and then she went to her own late model Cherokee, starting it up and then idling it until T.J. pulled out of the parking lot.

T.J.'s pace as he exited was slow.

Slow enough that it gave her yet another chance to see Fisher, the disapproval still stamped on his face as he observed them.

"Tell me again what happened?" she pressed, sensing there was something off about T.J.'s version of the speeding and accident.

"It was just an accident, Ma," he said, slouching negligently in his chair in the kitchen.

"Tell me again why you were speeding?"

His big hands, like those of Fisher, man's hands on a boy's body, flopped up and down before settling on the surface of the table. "I didn't mean to only... There was another car. It was fast. It kept getting in our face—"

"In your face? As in threatening you? Why didn't you pull over? Use your cell phone to call the police?" Macy asked as she rested her hands on the table where T.J. sat, leaning closer.

A glimmer of fear flickered across his features, impossible to miss. "No, not like that. You know like...challenging us. Trying to prove their car was better."

She understood about men and cars. Entire industries had been built about proving who was faster, better, fancier. She also understood about men and cars and girls.

"Sara was with you?"

Another small flinch rippled across his body and T.J. couldn't meet her gaze as he answered, "We had already dropped Sara off at the ranch."

She hadn't had time at the police station to ask Jewel

whether Sara had been home at the ranch when the call had come from Deputy Rawlings. She certainly would ask tomorrow because she was sure T.J. wasn't telling the truth.

"So you were drag racing? And because you were speeding, you couldn't stop when that car pulled out?"

An indifferent shrug greeted her queries, infuriating her, but she knew she had to keep her cool. Nothing would be gained by anger.

"You've already earned enough at the ranch to pay me back for the coach's mailbox. What you earn from now on will pay for the repairs to both cars and the speeding ticket. Do you understand?"

He nodded without hesitation, but never raised his gaze to meet hers.

"You're also grounded for a month. You come home after your work at the ranch. On the weekends, I'll have chores for you to do around the house. Understood?"

A shrug greeted her punishment.

"I'm going to bed. It's late and we both need to go to work tomorrow," she said, but she didn't want the night to end angrily.

She kneeled before her son, cradled his jaw with her hand and gently urged his face upward. Reluctantly, he met her gaze. "*You* are the most important thing in the world to me, T.J. You can trust me with anything. Anything," she said in the hopes of having him tell her the truth about what had really happened that night.

A sheen of tears glimmered in her son's eyes. He gulped, holding back emotion before he said, "I know, Mom. I love you."

"I love you," she said, sat up and hugged him, believing that all would be right with him as long as they still had love to bind them together.

* * *

She was a coward, she thought, not looking forward to speaking with Jewel about what had happened the night before. Because of that, and knowing Jewel's sweet tooth, she was on her way to Miss Sue's again for yet more sticky buns.

Luck was on her side as there was an empty parking space directly in front of Miss Sue's. But then she noticed that Fisher was once again sitting at a booth in the restaurant.

Didn't he ever eat at home? she wondered with irritation as she took a deep breath to fortify herself, exited the car and entered the cafe.

As she passed by the booth where he sat finishing up a mound of Miss Sue's scrambled eggs with bacon, cheese and hash browns, he met her gaze. Rebuke filled his green eyes and within her, annoyance built. At the counter, she forced a smile to her face as she ordered the sticky buns.

The waitress smiled warmly and offered her sympathies. "Boys will be boys, Macy. Don't let it get to you."

She nodded, but said nothing else. She also didn't turn to brave the rest of the people in the restaurant, although she sensed their stares as she waited. In a town the size of Esperanza, Miss Sue's was Information Central and everyone already knew about what had happened the night before.

Her sticky bun order came up to the counter. She paid quickly, eager to make her exit, but as she headed out, she noticed Fisher's attention was on her once again and something inside of her snapped.

In one smooth move, she slipped into the booth across from him, surprising him with her action. Calmly she said, "You don't know me or my son, so don't presume to judge us so quickly."

Fisher slowly put down his mug of coffee. Lacing his fingers together, he leaned forward and in soft tones said, "And I don't intend to get to know you…again. Once Jericho returns and I'm sure all is right with him, I'll be off and out of your way."

Out of her way, but also in harm's way, it occurred to her guiltily. "There's no need to rush back to the Army on my account."

He tossed up his hands in emphasis. "The Army is all I know and need. Discipline. Order. Respect."

The condemnation lashed at her once again. Discipline, order and respect clearly being things that he seemed to find lacking with her and her son. Sadly, she acknowledged that she, too, wished she had more of those traits in her life. Because of that, she tempered her response.

"I'm glad the military makes you happy. I hope you stay safe when you go back."

She didn't wait for a reply. She swept her box of sticky buns from the booth's table and hurried out the door.

In her Cherokee, she handed the box to T.J., who placed it in his lap and said, "What was that?"

"Excuse me?" she said as she pulled away from the curb.

"You and Captain Yates. It looked…intense," her son said and she realized that T.J. had seen everything through the plate glass window of Miss Sue's.

Striving for a neutral tone, she said, "Nothing important. I just asked him if he'd heard from Jericho. I expect he and Olivia will be back soon from their honeymoon."

T.J. snorted loudly and shook his head. "You're not a very good liar, Mom."

Her hands tightened on the wheel, but she said nothing else

which prompted T.J. to add, "Maybe you should practice what you preach. Maybe you should talk about what's up with you and Captain Yates."

What was up with her and Fisher was more than she suspected T.J. could handle at the moment. He'd been walking a very fine line lately and she was concerned that telling him the truth about Fisher would push him over the edge. If he crossed that line, she worried that the next trip to the sheriff's station would result in more than community service or a speeding ticket.

Because of that, she kept her silence as they drove toward the ranch.

T.J. also kept silent, guarding his own secrets she suspected since she still believed he was not telling her the whole truth about what had happened the night before.

At the ranch, it was Jewel who opened the door when they pulled up in the driveway. There was no mistaking the look on her boss's face that said she intended to get to the bottom of things.

Taking a deep breath, Macy braced herself as she approached the door to the ranch.

Chapter 7

The sticky buns became an after lunch treat as she joined Jewel and Ana in the shade at a patio table near the pool.

Jewel had opted to say little to the boys other than to assign them a mess of chores that would keep them busy until she intended to speak to them. That kept Sara with the other children rather than with her two new best friends. During their absence, the young girl retreated more deeply into her shell.

Ana's face was flushed by the midday heat as she slowly lowered herself into a chair at the table.

Macy placed a tall glass of milk before her, but two iced coffees before her spot and Jewel's. Then she set a sticky bun at each place before sitting beside Ana. Jewel came by a few minutes later after reminding the children in the pool about the rules.

Jewel's face was also flushed from the heat and wisps of

her short wavy brown hair curled around her face. Dark circles marred the fragile skin beneath her cocoa brown eyes.

"I'm sorry about last night. I know you couldn't have slept well afterward," she said.

Jewel nodded, her lips in a grim smile. "I didn't. The call about the accident brought back painful memories."

"You were in an accident?" Ana asked, leaning forward and examining Jewel's features.

Jewel looked away and gripped the glass of iced coffee. With her thumb, she wiped away the condensation on its surface and said, "My fiancé and I were in an accident on the night he proposed to me. He was killed. Although I survived, I lost the baby I was carrying."

"*Perdoname.* I didn't mean to pry," Ana replied and dipped her gaze downward to her own pregnant belly. Almost protectively, she ran her hand across the rounded mound.

"It's all right, Ana. You couldn't have known," Jewel reassured her. "I was lucky to have Joe and Meredith Colton by my side, otherwise I think I might have lost my mind."

"The Coltons seem like wonderful people," Macy chimed in.

Jewel nodded emphatically. "They are which is why I'm so happy that with Daniels being exposed and jailed, Joe's presidential campaign has taken off. His nomination seems like a sure thing now."

"Definitely. I can't imagine how Olivia must have felt when she regained her memory and realized it was Daniels who was trying to kill her," she said and a sudden screech from the pool snagged her attention, but it was only two of the kids engaged in a splashing match.

Jewel had also whipped around at the noise, obviously on the edge. But when she realized it was nothing serious, she returned her attention to her friends. "Olivia's lucky to have found Jericho only... How are you dealing with canceling the wedding? Are you—"

"Convinced it was the right thing to do. It wouldn't have been right for me and Jericho to be together. Even though we love each other as friends, he deserves more from a marriage and Olivia will give him that," she admitted. She grabbed her glass of iced coffee, light with milk and sweet with sugar and took a big gulp. The cool helped chase away some of the heat of midday.

"Do you think what happened with T.J. has to do with you and Jericho? That he's angry about it?" Jewel pressed and then quickly tacked on, "Or is it about Fisher Yates?"

The heat that pressed down on her now came from Jewel's inquiry and her own guilt about both the Yates men. "T.J. was upset with my decision to marry Jericho. He said he already had a dad."

"And Fisher?" her friend repeated.

She recalled T.J.'s words about how maybe she should talk about it, but she still wasn't ready to reveal the secret she had kept for so long. "That's a complicated story. Plus, I don't think that it has anything to do with the boys and last night."

Taking another bracing sip of her drink, she met Jewel's too perceptive gaze and realized her friend knew it was time to back off about Fisher. That she would talk only when she was good and ready. "I'm sorry about last night, Jewel. I've talked to T.J., but I feel as if he's only telling me part of what really happened."

"I've spoken with Joe as well, only..." Jewel hesitated and then picked up the sticky bun, tore off a piece. "There's something not right about their story," she finally said.

She nodded. "I agree, although I can't put my finger on what's wrong."

"They say they dropped Sara off, but I don't remember if she was home when I got the call. Do you, Ana?" Jewel asked.

Ana rolled her eyes upward as she tried to remember, but then shook her head. "I do not know. She was home later. When you and Joe came home."

"So maybe Sara was with them when the accident happened?" Macy said and glanced over at the young teen, who deprived of her two friends thanks to their chores, was sitting alone on the edge of the pool.

"If she was with the boys, why didn't the police see her?"

"And if she was with them, why would they lie about that?" Jewel wondered aloud.

"She has many secrets, I think," Ana added and absent-mindedly rubbed her hand over her belly once again.

"If she doesn't want to be found, she wouldn't want to be involved with the police," she said, considering the police were bound to discover who she was.

Jewel took another piece of sticky bun and motioned with it as she said, "But that doesn't explain why they were speeding, does it?"

"T.J. said there was another car out on the road. One that was challenging them to prove their car was better."

"A drag race? Joe says they didn't realize they were speeding. That they didn't see the other car until it was too late to stop," Jewel said, but then she turned in her seat to glance at the pool and Sara in particular. "I don't know what to believe, but my gut says it involves Sara."

"Boys, cars and girls. A familiar mix, don't you think?" she suggested, remembering her own teen years and the many times that mix had caused problems in town.

"I hope that's all it is," Jewel said, finishing off the last of her sticky bun and pointing at Macy's, which remained untouched before her. "If you're a true friend, you'll eat that," she said.

"Why is that?" she asked.

"Because otherwise I'm going to devour it and you don't want me to get fat." A hesitant smile spread across Jewel's face and Macy realized she was trying to lighten the moment.

As another playful shout came from the pool, Macy grabbed her sticky bun and with a playful snort said, "Fat. Right. That's why Deputy Rawlings is always making goo goo eyes at you."

"Goo goo eyes?" Ana asked, slightly confused by the expression.

"That means he's interested in Jewel," she explained and Ana smiled broadly, nodded with some spirit. "Definitely. I've seen how he looks at you whenever he visits."

The blush that now blossomed across Jewel's face wasn't from the warmth of the day. "I've tried my best to discourage him. I'm just not ready for another relationship."

Neither was she, although she had been hard-pressed to forget about Fisher during the day thanks to their encounter that morning. "Me, either," she chimed in and finished off the last of her sticky bun.

Ana was done as well with her treat and as Macy glanced at her watch, she realized their lunch hour was almost over.

"Do you want me to work with the older children on their study skills while Ana and the younger kids do some craft work?"

Jewel nodded. "I know school is still some time away, but it would be good for them to be ready. It'll also give me some time to talk to the boys."

The three women split up to finish their work for the day.

As she aided Sara and the two other older children with their study exercises, her mind was half on what was happening with Jewel, T.J. and Joe in the library where Jewel often met with the children privately.

It came as no surprise to her later that Jewel had not been able to get any other information from them.

It also didn't surprise her to see T.J., Joe and Sara huddled together by the corral later that afternoon, clearly engaged in some kind of animated conversation. As soon as the rest of the group neared in order to take some rides on Papa's Poppy, the conversation stopped.

Their actions worried her, but with T.J. grounded for a month due to the speeding and accident, the trio was unlikely to get into trouble anytime soon.

Anytime soon hopefully being long after Jericho had returned from his honeymoon and Fisher had left town.

She knew which Yates brother she could count on to help her and it sure wasn't Fisher, she thought.

Relative quiet ruled over dinner that night.

T.J. didn't have much to say about either his discussion with Jewel or what he, Joe and Sara were talking about at the corral.

In truth, she didn't push too hard for the information. If she did, T.J. would become even more tight-lipped and remind her that she had something she needed to get off her chest as well.

Namely Fisher.

She hadn't been able to get him out of her mind all day and as she slipped into bed that night, he once again invaded her dreams as if to remind her that she had been about to marry the wrong Yates brother.

* * *

A small crowd gathered around the steps of the church. Jewel and Ana. An assortment of Coltons. Jericho and a pregnant Olivia, her rounded belly larger than it had been just a few weeks before. Buck Yates stood beside them, a broad smile on his face.

As she neared the group, she stumbled on something and looked down.

She had stepped on the hem of her dress—her wedding dress.

Confused, she paused and stared back up at the gathering of friends and family, only everyone had disappeared, leaving only two people on the steps—Fisher and T.J.

T.J. looked solemn and too grown-up in his dark blue suit—the suit she had bought for him to wear for her wedding to Fisher.

No, not Fisher.

Jericho, she reminded herself, but as she stared at her son and the man standing next to him, she realized just how much T.J. looked like Fisher, his father.

It was there in the squareness of their jaws and the lean build of their bodies. T.J.'s hair was darker than hers, closer to Fisher's nearly black hair much like T.J.'s eyes were a mix of Fisher's green and her brown.

The physical similarities between the two men was undeniable.

She wondered why she hadn't seen it before. Why others hadn't seen it over the years. Suddenly, she realized everyone had gone.

Everyone except Fisher who stood there, lethally handsome in his Army uniform. The dark blue of the fabric intensified the green of his eyes while the fit of the jacket lovingly caressed the broad width of his shoulders and leanness of his waist.

She remembered those shoulders, she thought as she took a step toward him and the distance between them vanished.

Suddenly in his arms, she braced her hands against those strong shoulders only they were bare now beneath the palms of her hands much as she was now bare, the wedding dress having evaporated into the ether of her dreams.

His skin was warm against hers as he pressed her to his lean muscled body. A man's hard body, she thought, recalling the strength of him on the one night they had shared so long ago. Remembering the emotions he had roused that had shaken her to the core of her being.

She met his gaze, her own likely confused as she said, "I've never forgotten our one night."

"Neither have I," he said and lowered his forehead to rest against hers. His tones soft, he said, "Why did you marry Tim?"

She had loved Tim with all her heart. Loved him in a way that was different from how she felt for Fisher and yet…

She had loved Fisher as well after that night. And because of that emotion, she hadn't been able to ruin his life when she had heard of his enlistment and excitement to be leaving Esperanza.

At her hesitation, he smiled sadly and said, "Still not talking? You didn't want to talk after that night either."

No, she hadn't wanted to talk. She had wanted to show him how she cared in other ways and so she did that now, rising up the inch or so to press her lips to his.

Fisher groaned like a man in pain at that first touch, but then he answered her kiss, meeting her lips again and again. Tenderly breaching the seam of her mouth with his tongue to taste her. To unite them until every move and breath became as one between them and just kissing wasn't enough.

He gently lowered her to the ground and the softness of well-worn fabric, smelling like her mama's detergent, dragged her eyes open.

It was night out and they were lying on a blanket on the overlook, much as they had done eighteen years before.

The sky above them was a deep endless black dotted with hundreds of stars and a bright summer moon that silvered all below as it had so many years earlier.

As she met his gaze, he cupped her cheek and ran his thumb across the moistness his kisses had left behind on her lips.

"I never forgot that night," he said once again.

"Neither did I," she admitted and gave herself over to his loving.

Chapter 8

Macy bolted upright in bed, breathing heavily. Her body thrummed with unfulfilled desire.

She yanked a shaky hand through her hair, troubled about the dream. Troubled because it had hit too close to home regarding her feelings for Fisher.

No matter how hard she had tried to forget him during the last eighteen years, he had always been with her. In her brain and in her heart.

Tim had known and understood. Had realized that her love for him was strong and true, but that Fisher had touched a part of her that could not be his.

She had admired Tim for that and for claiming T.J. as his. It had allowed both her and Fisher to get on with their lives in the ways that both of them had wanted.

And what about T.J.? the niggling voice of guilt

reminded. What about Fisher not knowing he has a child? it lashed out.

Shaking her head as if to clear out that nagging voice, she slipped from bed and walked down the hall to T.J.'s room.

The door was open and as she peered at her sleeping son, the guilt flailed at her repeatedly. T.J.'s features were stamped with Fisher's, she thought again. If Fisher had stayed in town, or visited more often than during his occasional breaks between tours of duty, she would not have been able to keep her secret for so long.

It made her wonder why the other Yates men hadn't seen the resemblance, or if they had, why they hadn't said anything?

With such thoughts dragging at her, she returned to bed only to find sleep was impossible.

Grabbing her romance novel from her nightstand, she read, knowing it would give her the happily-ever-after that she seemed unable to find in her own life.

Fisher sat before the fireplace in his father's home, staring at the pile of logs ready to be lit when fall came and brought with it the cooler weather.

He had been tempted to light the fire tonight to chase away the chill from the jog he had decided to take earlier that evening. That chill had registered in his thirty-seven-year-old bones, he told himself, but the annoying voice in his head chastised him. Warned him that what he was feeling was something else.

Guilt, maybe?

The hurt look on Macy's face that morning had chased him throughout the day, especially when despite that hurt, she had wished him to stay safe.

Safe. A funny word.

For the eighteen years he had been in the military, he had regularly kept himself and his men safe. Not that there hadn't been injuries or times when he had thought he'd never see home again. But through it all he'd kept his head and made sure each and every man had come home alive.

Coming home being so important except…

He didn't feel safe here.

Being near Macy reminded him of all that his home lacked. Hell, it wasn't even his home, but his dad's, he thought, glancing around at the place where he had grown up and to where he returned after each tour of duty was over.

He rose from the couch and to the breakfast bar that separated the living room from the kitchen. A single bottle of bourbon sat on the bar and he poured himself a finger's worth of the alcohol and returned to sit before the fireplace.

After a bracing sip of the bourbon, he winced and considered what it would be like to have his own home. Wondered what it would be like to have someone like Macy to come home to. Not that Macy would be interested because she hadn't been interested eighteen years earlier.

Not to mention there was T.J. to consider.

As he had seen Macy and her son leave the police station the night before, he had thought, much as his brother and father had said, that what the boy needed was a strong man in his life to help set things straight.

He chuckled as amusement set in because he had no doubt that the headstrong and independent Macy would tan his hide for such a chauvinistic thought. Not to mention that it was ridiculous to consider that he might be that man. He wasn't the kind to settle down into the whole home and hearth thing.

Of course, his brother Jericho hadn't seemed like that kind of man either. He took another sip of the liquor, leaned his head back onto the couch cushions and considered his surprise at how happy his brother had looked marrying Olivia.

That look had confirmed to him that maybe his brother was the marrying type, but also that his brother's plan to wed Macy had been totally wrong from the outset. For starters, you didn't marry out of obligation and you sure shouldn't plan on having a platonic relationship with your wife.

A bit of anger built inside of him at both his brother and Macy at that thought. Macy for relying on her friendship to even consider the marriage and at his brother for agreeing to it, especially since he couldn't imagine lying next to Macy in bed and having it stay platonic.

His gut tightened at the thought of his kid brother making love to the only woman who had ever managed to break her way into his heart.

Since his mom had left, he hadn't had much faith in women and had sealed shut his heart…until Macy had somehow slipped through a crack.

Of course, after her abandonment, he had walled off his heart from hurt once again, but the memory of her had stayed locked behind those barriers. And now with her involvement with Jericho, it had roused all those old memories.

Slugging back the last dregs of the bourbon, he rose from the sofa, went to the kitchen and washed the glass. Slipped it into the dish drain sitting there holding an odd assortment of china and cutlery.

A single man's mix of mismatched items, he thought.

A woman would have made sure all the cutlery and plates were the same and that something wouldn't be sitting in the dish drain for days. It would be washed, dried and put away in anticipation of the next family meal.

Like when Macy and T.J. sat down to their next meal, he thought, but couldn't picture himself there beside them. She and T.J. had too many issues and it would be best for him to lay low until Jericho came home.

Once his brother returned, he would be back on his way to the Army, although he hadn't decided whether it would be to another tour of duty in the Middle East or the instructor's position at West Point.

The former was familiar, but he understood the importance of the latter. Even acknowledged how it could be a new adventure for him. A different mission.

Teaching up and coming officers was as significant as being out in the field with his men. After all, the nation needed excellent military men to lead and his many years of experience could help those cadets become better officers and save lives.

But as Fisher walked to his bedroom—the same one in which he'd slept as a child—he wondered if he would grow bored with living in one place and having the same basic daily routine. For nearly eighteen years he'd avoided that and he couldn't imagine changing now unless...

It would take something really special for that kind of change, he realized as he stared at his cold and lonely single bed.

Fisher drove from his mind the picture of Macy waiting for him in that bed because he feared that maybe Macy could be that something really special to change his life.

As he undressed and slipped beneath the chilly sheets, he reminded himself that Macy needed more than a man in her life. Her son needed a father figure and once again it occurred to him that he wasn't the right man for that job.

But as he drifted off to sleep, visions of her seeped into his dreams, reminding him of just how much he was missing in life.

Chapter 9

Macy awoke tired and grumpy. Her night's sleep—or lack of—had been dominated by thoughts of both Fisher and T.J.

None of her deliberations had been good, she thought as she and T.J. drove to the ranch. But then blushed as she remembered her dreams of making love with Fisher.

Of course, any pleasure had been wiped out by her son's surly mood. That morning he had complained about how hard he and Joe had worked the day before until she had pointedly reminded him of how much it had cost for the speeding ticket and repairs.

His cold silence had replaced the complaints during the short ride to the ranch.

When they entered the house to share breakfast with the others, he became slightly more animated, taking a spot by Joe and Sara and striking up a conversation with them.

She watched their camaraderie and was more convinced than ever that Sara had something to do with the speeding and accident.

Her intuition was confirmed when she sat with Ana and Jewel and her boss leaned over and said, "Some of the kids mentioned that they thought Sara wasn't home when the Sheriff phoned about the accident."

"She was with the boys?" Ana asked softly, keeping her tone low so that the conversation would remain with them.

"I thought so. Boys, cars and girls just seem to create problems when you mix them together," Jewel replied and took a sip of her coffee.

Macy ran a finger along the rim of her cup as she considered Jewel's words, so similar to the thoughts she'd had herself. T.J. had been working hard on restoring the muscle car and quite proud of not only the vehicle's looks, but the power beneath the hood. And even though she had thought that, she also sensed there was more to it.

Meeting her boss's gaze, she said, "That may be true, but I would feel a lot more comfortable if we knew more about Sara. About why she's here and why all three of them would be lying about her being with them that night."

Jewel paused with her mug in midair, then slowly lowered it to the table. "You know the Hopechest policy. We offer refuge without qualification. Without making any demands that our residents reveal anything."

She was well aware of the Hopechest policy. They had taken in each of the children and even Ana without question.

She nodded and said nothing else of it as they finished breakfast, instead turning to a discussion of what Jewel wanted them to do that day with the children. As she had done the day before, her boss piled on a load of chores for the two boys and after breakfast, they all went their separate ways.

Despite the work assigned to them, she noticed that the two boys managed to spend their free time with Sara. At the midday lunch break and then again during the afternoon rides at the corral, T.J. and Joe were engaged with Sara, their heads bent together in discussion.

She had hoped to speak to T.J. about it on their way home, but he was exhausted and irritated once again, not to mention smelly from mucking out the mare's stall. Wrinkling her nose, she said, "Please shower while I make dinner."

He yanked one iPod earpiece out and angry music blared from it as he faced her. "What if I'm not hungry?"

Considering how hard he had been working, she couldn't imagine him not needing to refuel his growing body, but she wouldn't get into a war of words with him.

"Then I'll eat alone."

His mouth flopped up and down like that of one of the sunfish they used to pull out of the small pond behind the high school, but he said nothing else.

He did shower as she had asked and met her at the dinner table where he silently shoveled in the burger and fries she had made. He even deigned to sit with her for a slice of a home-baked apple pie, à la mode of course.

But after that, he excused himself, saying that he was tired and planned on going to bed early.

She didn't argue with him, recognizing that the space might help him get over his pique.

After he left the kitchen, she turned on the small television tucked into a corner cabinet and took her time cleaning up. Washing the pans and dishes by hand, slowly and methodically since she found the simple work relieved her mind of thinking of more complex things.

It was barely eight when she finished, went up the stairs and passed by the door of T.J.'s room. His door was ajar and she peered within. As her son had said, he was in bed and asleep.

Relieved at the momentary peace that his slumber brought, she retired to her room where she changed into her pajamas, slipped beneath the covers and grabbed her book, intending to finish it.

A few hours passed and she was near the end of the novel when she thought she heard a noise.

T.J.? she wondered and eased from her bed to check on him.

He was still tucked safely in bed and she returned to her own, finished off the last few pages, smiling at the ending.

It was with those happy thoughts that she turned off her light and lay down to sleep.

She drifted off in that blissful state, her mind turning to thoughts of happier times. With T.J. and her husband Tim before the cancer had robbed him of life. With Fisher on the one night that had forever changed her destiny.

Her memories muddled together in dreams, becoming ones of her, Fisher and T.J. together until the phone rang beside her, rudely pulling her from her dreams.

Barely awake, she grabbed the phone, raking her sleep-tousled hair away from her face as she realized that it was barely six in the morning.

No good news at such an hour.

"Macy?"

It was Jewel on the line and she came instantly awake.

"What's wrong, Jewel?"

"Sara's missing."

* * *

The police combed every inch of the ranch house looking for clues as to Sara's disappearance.

They questioned everyone on the ranch, including T.J. and Joe who unfortunately, had little to offer as to Sara's possible whereabouts or why she would run away from the ranch.

When the police had left, Jewel and she had questioned the two teens once again, but they had little information to offer. Sadly, she knew as did Jewel that the two boys were being evasive. Despite that, hope remained within her that T.J. was not involved. He had eaten dinner with her and gone to bed early. She had seen him in his bed last night not just once, but twice.

Twice because she had heard something, she thought.

As she watched T.J. and Joe during the afternoon break, she wondered what it was that she had heard. If there had been more to it that she hadn't realized.

Her worst fears were confirmed when Deputy Rawlings returned to the ranch shortly after four.

As he walked toward the corral where they were offering the children rides on Papa's Poppy, she understood it was no social visit and so did the children. They stopped what they were doing and huddled together by the split rail fence. In the corral, T.J. and Joe helped the one child down from the horse and then also stood there, clearly anxious.

Deputy Rawlings dipped his head as she and Jewel approached him and removed his hat. "Miss Jewel. Miss Macy."

"Do you have news, Adam?" she asked, striving for a friendly tone.

He looked down for a moment, seemingly ashamed before he lifted his face and looked at her directly. "We started asking some of the Hopechest's neighbors if they had seen anything."

He continued with his report, his tone hesitant. "About a half mile up the road, one of the neighbors heard a car door slam. It was late so she looked out the window to see who it was."

A cold chill filled her as he motioned to T.J. and Joe with his hat. "She saw a young girl getting into a car with a dented front fender. From her description of the girl it seemed like it could be Sara. When we showed her pictures of the boys, she picked T.J."

Jewel laid a hand on her shoulder and stepped closer in a show of support. "You don't think T.J. had anything to do with—"

"I'm afraid I'll have to take him into custody. Ask him a few questions and find out why one of your neighbors thinks that she saw him last night with Sara."

"Can't you just question him here?" she said and he shook his head.

"There's procedures to follow and—"

"Jericho wouldn't do this," she insisted.

A strong flush of color filled his cheeks and a muscle ticked along his jaw. "Sheriff Yates isn't here and he left me in charge. There's procedures I have to follow, Mrs. Ward."

Without waiting for her, he once again motioned to the boys and called out, "T.J. I need you to come with me, son."

Her stomach clenched as she waited, hoping that he would be obedient. That he wouldn't give the deputy anything else to use as ammunition against him.

Blessedly, he did just what Deputy Rawlings asked.

With a worried look that he shot at Joe, who clapped him on the back, T.J. turned the reins of the horse over to his friend and walked to the edge of the corral. Easing beneath one of the rails of the fence, he approached the officer and said, "I haven't done anything wrong."

But she realized that with those words, he also wasn't denying any involvement with Sara's disappearance.

"Thank you for cooperating, son."

"I'm not your son," T.J. said with gritted teeth.

Deputy Rawlings nodded, laid a hand on T.J.'s shoulder and walked him around the side of the house toward the driveway.

Macy glanced at Jewel out of the corner of her eye and said, "I need to follow them into town. Find out what Adam plans to do."

Jewel squeezed her shoulder reassuringly. "I'll go with—"

"No, you stay here. The kids will need you to talk about this and so will Joe," she immediately said, appreciating Jewel's offer. The children were clearly upset by what was happening which was understandable. Some of them may have had run-ins with the law or been disappointed with the systems put in place to protect them. They would need Jewel's reassurance about what was happening.

"I'll call you as soon as I know anything more," she added and without waiting, rushed after T.J. and the police officer.

As she caught up to them, Deputy Rawlings eased T.J. into the backseat of the cruiser, then he took the wheel.

Macy quickly got settled in her own car and followed a safe distance behind the cruiser. She followed it into the parking lot for the police station and got out of her car, but as she headed toward the door, Deputy Rawlings stopped and faced her.

"It might be best for you to go get a coffee while T.J. and I talk."

She thought about her son being interrogated by the officer. She didn't like the thought of it, but she also didn't want to anger the deputy. Taking a deep breath, she looked away and realized Fisher and his dad were across the street in front of Miss Sue's.

They watched intently, clearly aware that something was up. A condemning look immediately came to Fisher's face, but Buck's features were more supportive. A second later, the older man took a step toward them and after some initial hesitation, Fisher followed his dad.

Shaking her head, she returned her attention to the police officer and decided to voice her concerns. "I'm not sure it's such a good idea that T.J. speak to you alone."

Chapter 10

Deputy Rawlings' lips tightened into an ascetic line as he ripped off his hat, frustration and anger evident in every brusque movement. "Why do you want to make this difficult? I'm not taking T.J. into custody. I just want to ask him a few simple questions."

"Is there a problem, Macy?" Buck Yates asked as he stood beside her.

She glanced up at Buck, avoiding Fisher when he took a spot just to the right of his dad. "One of the teens has gone missing from the ranch and Deputy Rawlings wants to speak to T.J. about it."

Buck nodded and pushed his hat back, adopting a stance that was more casual than that of the officer. "I'm sure the deputy understands how troubling this is for both you and T.J. That he needs to handle this carefully. Right, Deputy?"

A muscle clenched along the officer's jaw, but he nodded slowly. "Certainly, Buck. I know how to deal with this."

"Good. How about you join Fisher and me for dinner, Macy? Give the deputy and T.J. some time just to chat."

Protest gathered within her, ready to erupt, but Buck slipped his arm around her shoulders and hugged her so she kept her tongue. When the deputy took her son away, she forced a weak smile at the older man.

"Thank you for the invite, Buck, but I'm not sure I could eat a thing right now."

"I won't take no for an answer," he said and applied gentle pressure to turn her around. He guided her in the direction of Miss Sue's, Fisher quietly following behind them.

Inside the restaurant they were quickly seated at a booth. Buck took the one bench and sat in the middle, giving her no option but to slide along the vinyl of the other booth bench until Fisher could sit beside her.

The waitress came over and handed them menus.

She had intended not to take one, lacking any appetite, but Buck's half-lidded look brooked no disagreement.

After a short perusal of the menu, she ordered a soup and a half of a fresh roasted turkey sandwich, earning a satisfied nod from the older man.

Neither Fisher nor he seemed to have any problem with their appetites since they ordered the blue plate specials, which included not only the soup of the day, but chicken-fried steak with white gravy, squash and cheese casserole, green beans and a choice of dessert.

After taking their orders, the waitress brought over tall glasses of iced tea, a dish of summer slaw and a basket heaped with warm corn bread and sweet cream butter.

The enticing smell of the corn bread made her stomach growl. She placed a hand above her belly, but Fisher picked up the basket and offered it to her. "Would you like some?"

She smiled and thanked him. After buttering the corn bread, she took a bite and sighed as the dulcet flavors of the corn and butter filled her mouth.

"This is good," she said, but then quickly added, "but not as good as that jalapeño corn bread you used to make for us when we were kids, Buck."

"That was really tasty with your five alarm chili, Pa," Fisher said, but then stuffed a big piece of buttered corn bread in his mouth.

Buck laughed and forked some of the summer slaw onto his bread dish. "The four of you could sure eat," he said with a chuckle.

Fisher nodded, recalling the many nights that Macy and Tim had joined his family for a meal. "Those were good times."

"Yes, they were," Macy said. A sad sigh followed, however.

"It'll be okay, darlin'. Don't worry about T.J.," Buck offered, but Macy dipped her head down until her chin was nearly burrowing a hole in her chest.

Upset by her dismay, Fisher reached beneath the table and laid his hand over hers. "It will be okay," he also reassured.

With a long inhale and a sniffle, Macy nodded. "Yes, it will be okay. I'll make it okay."

He had no doubt of her sincerity, but worried about whether she could make good on it. T.J. seemed to be bringing her nothing but trouble and possibly the boy needed a man's influence in his life. A man who would be there for him.

When the waitress brought their meals, he withdrew his

hand from hers and they all dug into their dinners, hunger bringing a long stretch of quiet to the table.

Macy finished her meal quickly, but he and his dad had quite a lot to eat. While he ate, he offered Macy a small piece of his steak and she tried it, murmured her approval. Slowly he and his father finished their meals and by the time dessert came, they convinced Macy to get some peach cobbler.

When they were finally finished, Macy offered to pay to thank them for their company, but his father insisted it was their treat and that they should do it more often.

"I'd like that, Buck," she said.

Then something inside of him—something Fisher didn't understand and didn't want to acknowledge—had him saying, "I'll go with you to the sheriff's office."

Her mouth opened as she prepared to refuse him, but then she abruptly snapped it shut. "I'd appreciate that," she said instead.

In front of the restaurant she hugged Buck and thanked him again before the two of them silently walked side by side to the sheriff's office.

Inside the police station, one of the other deputies manned the front desk. As he realized who had entered, he sheepishly glanced down at the papers on his desk, but Fisher wasn't about to be dissuaded.

"You know me better than that, Bill. Where's Deputy Rawlings?"

Bill shuffled the papers into order before addressing them. "Deputy Rawlings is still with the suspect."

"The suspect?" Macy nearly croaked. "When did he become a suspect?"

Before the other man could answer, Deputy Rawlings stepped from one of the back rooms. He grimaced when he noticed them standing by the front desk, but swaggered over, his shoulders thrown back. Hands cocked on his hips.

"Macy. Fisher," he said with a curt nod.

"Evening, Adam. I came to see when I could take T.J. home," she said, bracing her hands along the edge of the front desk.

Adam looped his thumbs through his belt loops and swayed side to side on his feet for a moment. "I'm sorry, but I've decided to keep T.J. overnight while we continue our investigations."

The other deputy rose from the desk, wisely making himself absent for the discussion that would follow.

"Excuse me," Macy said, her voice rising with each syllable, prompting Fisher to reach over and place his hand on her shoulder to try to calm her.

"We need to be sure there's no foul play," the deputy said and beneath his hand, the tension escalated in Macy's body.

"Come on now, Adam. There's no reason—"

"A young girl is missing. We have a witness who claims to have seen your son with her on the night she disappeared."

Macy inched up on her toes, ready to erupt, but he applied gentle pressure to keep her in control. Macy didn't normally have a temper, but when it involved her family, he didn't doubt that she would tenaciously defend her son.

"You know Jericho wouldn't do this," she urged and he had no doubt about that. Jericho would not be handling this situation as badly as Deputy Rawlings, but he could see that the man was not responding well to being challenged.

He opted for a different approach, hoping that he could calm the deputy until his brother returned in a day or two. "No one doubts your concerns, Deputy, but wouldn't it be possible to release T.J. into his mother's custody? I'm sure she can—"

"Handle him?" The deputy chuckled harshly and shook his

head. "Mrs. Ward hasn't done a very good job of controlling T.J. so far. Until we know that there's been no foul play, I'm going to hold him overnight. Maybe even longer."

Macy's body trembled beneath his hand, but she somehow kept her cool. "Please don't do this, Adam. I promise to bring T.J. back in the morning—"

"I don't think so," the deputy said and Fisher was about to jump in and offer his assurances, but bit the words back. He knew little about T.J. other than that both his brother and dad believed he was good, but confused. Worse yet, he knew nothing about how to deal with the boy and even if he did…

He would be gone in another couple of weeks.

Becoming involved in their lives not only made little sense, it would be cruel since he could promise nothing of permanence. But he needed to help Macy now.

"Let's go, Macy. We'll come back in the morning."

Macy shot a worried look at him and while glancing her way, he said, "The deputy knows what he needs to do. He'll take good care of T.J."

He faced the other man and left no doubt about his words. "You will take good care, right?"

Adam stalked the remaining distance to the front desk and leaned over the barrier toward him. "That's not a threat, is it?"

"Just a reminder," he said, dipped his head and smiled, making sure that the other man understood it was a promise of what might happen if T.J. wasn't cared for. Then he urged Macy back from the desk. "We'll see you bright and early, Adam. Have a nice night."

Slipping his arm completely around Macy's shoulders, he steered her out the door of the station and onto the steps, where she shrugged off his touch and wrapped her arms around herself.

"Jericho wouldn't do this. He would know that T.J. could never hurt that girl," she said.

"But is T.J. involved in her disappearance?" Fisher asked, but as Macy's face paled at his words, he cursed beneath his breath.

"I'm sorry," he said and took her into his arms.

She was tense at first, but then she slowly relaxed and embraced him. Laying the side of her face on his chest, she said, "Thank you. I was a little tired of going it alone."

He suspected that up until her cockamamie idea to marry Jericho, she had been going it alone ever since Tim's death nearly six years earlier.

As she raised her face and her brown eyes, shimmering with unshed tears met his, he wanted to tell her that she didn't need to go it alone anymore. That he would be there for her, but he couldn't. But he also couldn't resist the pull of that emotional gaze or the desire to soothe the spot on her lower lip that she was worrying with her teeth.

He bent his head as she rose up on tiptoe. Licked the abused spot on her lower lip before covering her mouth with his.

She pressed into him, cupping the back of his head with her hand and he dug his fingers into the silky lushness of her shoulder-length brown hair.

When she opened her mouth to his, he pressed on, sliding his tongue along the perfect edge of her teeth before dancing it against her tongue. He wrapped his one arm beneath her buttocks and brought her full against him and with that dangerous full body contact, sanity returned.

They pulled apart abruptly, both of them breathing hard and obviously shocked by the intensity of the emotion they had unleashed with one simple embrace.

"Macy, I'm—"

She raised her hands to stop him. "Please don't say you're sorry because I'm not. There's no need for apologies or regrets. All I want to say is thank you for being here for me."

He dragged a hand through the short-cropped strands of his hair and held back on telling her what he wanted—that he wanted her again. Wanted her next to him. Wanted her lips beneath his, opening to his invasion. Inviting him to take it further.

Instead, he took a deep breath and stuffed the tips of his fingers into the pockets of his snug jeans to keep from reaching for her again.

"You're welcome. I'll see you home."

She wrapped her arms around herself once more and shook her head roughly, sending her hair into movement with the action. "You don't need to do that—"

"I do. Until Jericho is home, I want to make sure you're okay."

She looked away then, but he couldn't fail to see the tear as it slipped down her face and she said, "I understand, Fisher. I won't mistake what just happened for anything else."

He longed to take her into his arms and shake her until she did understand, only he wasn't sure he knew why they were both standing there, trembling with desire. Hungry for another taste, but fighting it.

Because of that confusion, he said, "How about I just watch you walk to your car. If you need me in the morning—"

"I'll call," she said, but as she walked away, he understood that she wouldn't.

Chapter 11

Macy spent the night tossing and turning, worried not only about T.J., but about the kiss that shouldn't have happened. The kiss that had rocked her world, reminding her how Fisher continued to move her. That she was still immensely attracted to him.

But she wouldn't call him.

Her life was complicated enough without adding Fisher to the mix. But the little voice in her head kept buzzing in warning. Guilting her that Fisher should know T.J. was his son. Urging her to explore the emotions he roused.

She ignored that stubborn buzz and focused on what she had to do that morning.

Rising early, she made herself some coffee, but was too nervous to eat. After showering, she phoned Jewel and asked for the day off so she could head to the sheriff's office to deal with Deputy Rawlings and T.J.

Sympathetic and supportive, her boss offered to meet her there to help in whatever way she could, but Macy couldn't accept it. She needed to deal with her problems on her own, much as she had since Tim's death.

With that focus, she rushed to the sheriff's office in the hopes of securing T.J.'s release.

Bill was at the front desk again, looking as uncomfortable as he had the night before.

"Good morning, Macy," he said, rose and held up his coffee mug. "Can I get you a cup?"

"Will I be here long enough to need one?" she said with a forced smile.

"I hope not. Let me go get Deputy Rawlings." He walked away, cup in hand, and to one of the offices, where he knocked.

Someone ripped the door open and Bill jumped back.

Deputy Rawlings stepped out from the office. As he realized she was there, he tempered his attitude. He walked to the front desk and swung open the waist-high door in invitation.

"Why don't you join me in my office?" he said and held his hand out.

"Can I take T.J. home now?" she asked as she passed by him and walked toward his office.

"Let's discuss this in private," the deputy replied, his tone obviously annoyed.

She wondered why they needed privacy much like she was still questioning why it had been necessary to keep T.J. overnight. She guarded her tongue since it would not accomplish anything if she lost her cool.

In his office, she sat before his desk and kept quiet, waiting for him to set the tone of the discussion.

He leaned back in his chair and laced his fingers together

on his flat stomach. "I spoke to T.J. at length yesterday. He clearly knows more about Sara's disappearance than he's saying, Macy."

"Sara and he are friends, Adam. He wouldn't do anything to hurt her. If anything, he's probably trying to protect her."

"I don't doubt that. In fact, our investigations so far seem to indicate that there isn't any foul play." He shot forward in the chair, opened a file on his desk and quickly moved some papers around.

"At least a week ago, Sara may have been at a local honky tonk about ten miles from here—the Amarillo Rose. One of the bartenders remembers a young girl being there and getting into a truck with someone."

She shifted to the edge of her seat and said, "So it's possible she's gone off with the same person again?"

The deputy shook his head and chuckled harshly. "Could be, although I'd put my money on T.J. But there's nothing so far that says she didn't go willingly or that any harm has come to her. Because of that, I'm going to let T.J. go—"

"Thank you," she said and popped up out of her chair, eager to go get her son.

Deputy Rawlings picked up his hands and waved for her to sit back down. "Easy now, Macy. Don't be in a rush because even though I'm letting T.J. go for now, you need to keep an eye on him. Make sure that if he knows anything about Sara, he lets us know before something bad does happen."

As angry as she was at the deputy's heavy-handed tactics, she couldn't argue with what he was asking. "If I find out anything, you'll be the first to know."

"Good to hear. I'll go get T.J. Why don't you meet us out front?"

Dismissed, she rose and headed to where Bill sat at the desk, sipping his coffee. As she approached, he said, "So you're taking T.J.?"

"I am," she answered, grasping the handles of her purse before her.

The sound of metal grating against metal snagged her attention—the jail cell opening. A second later, her son popped out, looking tired and haggard. As he saw her waiting for him, however, a smile quickly flashed across his face before he controlled it. He walked toward her slowly, hesitant, but when he stood before her, she reached out and hugged him hard. His body relaxed and he returned the embrace.

"We're going home, T.J."

She stepped away, but kept one arm around his shoulders, reluctant to lose contact with her son.

He didn't battle her but kept close to her side as they walked out the door of the sheriff's station.

She shot her son a sidelong glance. Relief washed over her as he met her gaze and another timid smile blossomed on his face. Everything would be okay, she thought until she nearly walked into the man standing before them on the steps of the sheriff's station.

Fisher.

In wickedly tight blue jeans, a chambray shirt that hugged his lean chest and abs, and a black Stetson that made his green eyes pop brightly in the morning sun.

"Fisher," she said out loud, a little more breathlessly than she liked.

"What are you doing here?" T.J. said and came to stand before her, placing himself between her and Fisher in an obviously protective gesture.

She placed her hand on T.J.'s shoulder and urged him back to her side. "Fisher and his dad were nice enough to keep me company last night. We had dinner together at Miss Sue's while I waited to see if Deputy Rawlings would let you go home."

T.J.'s mouth quirked with displeasure before he mustered some politeness. "Thank you for taking care of my mom."

Fisher seemed taken aback by the unexpected gratitude, but quickly recovered. "My pleasure. I'm sure Jericho would have done the same if he were here."

Disappointment stung her ego followed by confusion at the disappointment. Snagging her keys from her purse, she handed them to T.J. and pointed to where her car was parked across the street.

"Fisher and I need a moment alone. Why don't you go wait by the car for me?"

T.J. nodded, but before he left, he chanced an assessing look at Fisher. Then he did as she had asked, walking down the steps of the sheriff's office and to the corner, where he waited for the light to change so he could cross.

Macy shifted her attention to Fisher. "What are you doing here?"

He shrugged, looked away and dragged off his hat, bouncing it back and forth in his hands. With his head hanging down, he said, "I wish I knew."

She wished she knew as well and was about to press him for another answer when the squeal of tires rent the air. Loud, harsh and angry.

Both she and Fisher whirled toward the sound in time to see a large black sedan lurch wildly toward T.J. as he was crossing the street. Smoke came off one of the tires as the car burned rubber with the driver's haste to pick up speed.

"T.J.," they both shouted in unison and sprinted toward him, intent on getting him out of the path of the oncoming car.

He had noticed the car as well, but for a moment he stood there, stunned as the vehicle accelerated toward him. Then in a blur, he raced for the side of the street, trying to avoid the sedan which made no attempt to avert hitting him. If anything, it picked up speed, veering toward where T.J. had run to escape.

At the last minute, her son sidestepped the car like a matador might a bull as the vehicle traveled past him, but it still struck him a glancing blow. He flew into the air and against one of the parked cars as the sedan hurtled down the road, its engine racing as it continued to pick up speed.

She and Fisher rushed to where T.J. lay sprawled in the street as did a number of other pedestrians who had witnessed the accident.

When they reached his side, T.J. was attempting to rise, but Fisher laid a gentle hand on his shoulder. "Stay down, son. You could have some broken bones."

T.J. didn't argue, clearly dazed. A large gash on his temple bled profusely and he had a number of other cuts and scrapes along his face and arms.

Her hands shook as she passed a hand along T.J.'s forehead. As she glanced up the block, she noticed the flashing lights of an approaching ambulance and it filled her with relief. "Take it easy. Help will be here soon."

T.J. nodded, but even that small action seemed to hurt. He closed his eyes and lay there quietly, his face pale, frightening her.

Fisher sensed her fear. He placed his hand at the nape of her neck to steady her and said, "Don't worry. He'll be fine."

She sucked in a shaky scared breath and it rocked him all

the way to his gut. He wanted to make her feel better, but he was failing miserably.

Luckily, the EMTs arrived a second later and urged them both to move away.

He kept his contact with her as she stood there, arms wrapped around her waist. Her body tight with anxiety as they waited for some kind of word from the paramedics.

The young man finally looked up at them over his shoulder. "Nothing serious from what I can see, but we'll take him to the hospital just to confirm that."

The EMT quickly had the rest of his crew getting T.J. ready for transport. At the periphery of his vision, he noticed that Deputy Rawlings and one other officer were talking to the crowd, getting witness statements, he assumed. He wondered if anyone had gotten the license plate number. He had been too rattled to think about it, which shocked him. He was a man of action and trained to stay in control in stressful situations.

That he had lost that control scared him more than he wanted to admit.

But despite that, he knew he had to be in charge now for Macy and her son.

As the paramedics finished getting T.J. on a gurney, he took command. "Can his mother go with him in the ambulance?"

The EMT nodded. "Yes, but there's only room for your wife, sir."

"I'll follow in the car, Macy," he said and she nodded, murmured a strained, "Thanks."

He stood by her until T.J. was loaded into the ambulance and then he helped her climb up into the back. One of the paramedics came by and closed the door of the ambulance, leaving him standing there awkwardly until the sirens kicked in, reminding him he had something to do.

He had to follow them to the hospital and be there for them.

He had to do that, but not because it was what Jericho would have done.

He had to do it because his heart told him it was the right thing to do.

Chapter 12

Macy held T.J.'s hand as the paramedic placed a temporary bandage on the cut along his temple. When he was done, he strapped T.J.'s head in place to keep it from moving during the drive.

Apparently comfortable that T.J. didn't have any major injuries, the paramedic slipped into the seat beside the driver and left them alone in the back of the ambulance.

"How are you feeling?" she asked.

"A little sore, but I'll be okay," he said and squeezed her hand.

Macy thought back to the moment when she had heard the squeal of the tires and the car hurtled forward toward T.J. The fear of that moment fled, replaced by questions.

"I didn't recognize the car, did you?" Esperanza was a small town and almost everyone knew what kind of car everyone else drove.

"I didn't," her son replied, but something in his voice didn't ring true.

"Do you recollect anything about the car? The make or model? Did you see the face of the driver?"

"No, Ma. I was too busy trying not to get run over," he answered, the tone of his voice part annoyed but a greater part evasive.

"Are you sure—"

"I'm sure I was trying to get out of the way," he shot back and withdrew his hand from hers, bringing it to rest on his flat belly.

She focused on that hand, skinned along the knuckles. Drops of blood had congealed at various spots and there were more abrasions on his other hand. As she swept her gaze up and down his body, she noticed the angry road rash along one arm, from his elbow down to mid-forearm.

In her brain came the recollection of the low thud as the car caught him along one hip and he went flying, smacking into another car before falling to roll along the ground from the impact of the blow. A chill took hold in her center and she tried picturing the sedan again. Closed her eyes and attempted to remember what she could about the car, but it had all happened too fast.

The image of the vehicle was just a black blur as it sped toward T.J.

She was sure of that. The car had intended to hit her son. She had no uncertainty about that which made her wonder why T.J. might be lying to protect someone who had tried to hurt him.

The ride to the nearby hospital was blessedly short and the emergency room relatively empty. It didn't take long for them to examine T.J. and determine that there were no broken bones or a concussion. Although he would be bruised in a number of spots, especially along the one leg where the car had clipped him, there was no reason for the doctors to admit him.

Macy sighed with relief as the doctor made that pronouncement and finished sealing the cut on T.J.'s head with some butterfly bandages before taping a gauze pad over the wound. Another large bandage covered the road rash that they had cleaned while yet more gauze was wrapped around the knuckles on both hands.

As T.J. noticed her examining his various injuries, he barked out a short laugh and said, "You should see the other guy."

She chuckled and embraced him as he sat on the edge of the bed. "I was so scared."

"I'm okay, Mom. Really."

When she stepped away, he eased from the bed to stand upright, wincing as he put pressure on the leg which had taken the brunt of the hit from the car. It took him a moment to fully straighten and his first step was a little gimpy until he seemed to stretch out a kink.

With her arm around his shoulders, they walked out into the emergency room waiting area.

Fisher sat there, bouncing his black hat in his hand. He shot up out of the chair when he saw them and approached. Grimacing as he noted the bandages on T.J., he forced a smile and said, "I hope the other guy looks worse."

To her surprise, T.J. grinned and nodded. "He does."

Fisher motioned to the exit. "I brought your car from town. I'll go get it and drive you home."

The accident had rattled her nerves and having Fisher drive them would be a welcome respite. Concern remained about why someone would try to hurt T.J. and why he would cover up the fact that he might know who was responsible. As she and T.J. followed Fisher out of the hospital, she realized that she needed to tell someone about what was up with T.J. Needed to confide in someone who could help her deal with the problem.

As she watched Fisher pull up to the curb and saw how carefully he handled getting a sore T.J. into the car, she realized that Fisher might just be the someone she needed.

At seventeen, T.J. wouldn't have normally needed her to get him settled in bed, but he was aching enough now to require her assistance. She helped him take off his jeans. Managed to control her reaction at the sight of the large bruise which had already formed along his hip and thigh in addition to the smaller purpling marks along his other leg and ribs.

"Get some rest," she urged as she tucked him beneath the covers.

He nodded and closed his eyes, obviously drained by the events of the day.

She walked into the hall and left his door open, wanting to be able to hear him if he needed anything. She began to walk down the stairs, but paused a few steps down, peering through the open doorway of his room just to check on him again.

He seemed to be asleep already.

She breathed a sigh of relief that his injuries had been so minimal and finished her walk down the stairs. At the landing, she proceeded a few more steps and then turned into the kitchen.

Fisher stood at the counter by the coffee machine, pouring water into it. He slipped in a filter and then the coffee. Hit the button to get it going.

His actions were so domestic that it seemed incongruous

until she remembered how often she had seen Jericho do the same thing both in her home and his. They had grown up in a household full of men and such routine activities would likely be almost second nature to them.

She allowed herself the pleasure of watching him finish up the task, his movements sure and totally comfortable. Totally masculine. When he finished, he turned and realized she was standing there.

Fisher leaned back against the counter while he examined Macy. She appeared in control and he admired her strength in the midst of yet another crisis. Her strength being one of the things that had always attracted him.

"How's he doing?"

"Tired and sore. He's already fast asleep," she said and went to the small island in the middle of the kitchen, bent and retrieved two mugs and a sugar bowl which she placed on top of the island counter.

"And you?" he asked, raising one brow to emphasize the question.

She braced her hands on the edge of the counter, suddenly uneasy it seemed to him. She took a deep breath, held it before releasing it in a rush. Then she met his gaze directly and said, "I need your help."

"Just what kind of help?" he asked and from the corner of his eye he noticed that the pot of coffee was almost done. He took it from the machine, walked over and poured them both a cup of coffee.

She picked up the mug, her hands slightly shaky. She blew on the coffee and took a sip before placing the mug down. Bracing her hands on the counter once again, she looked away and said, "I think T.J. knows who was driving the car that hit him, but he's not admitting it. Normally I would have asked Jericho—"

"I'm not standing in for my brother, Macy. I'm not Jericho."

Her head whipped up and she nailed him with her gaze. "You're right that you're nothing like your brother. But you can't refuse to help."

He snorted and shifted his brow ever higher. "Really? Please tell me why I can't refuse."

No sign of emotion or distress marked her face as she said, "Because T.J. is your son."

Chapter 13

Sucker-punched.

That was the only way to describe how he was feeling.

She had sucker-punched him years ago with her first kiss and then again the night they'd made love.

Now she had done it again.

"Excuse me?" He came round the corner of the island until he stood directly beside her. She had looked away immediately after her pronouncement. Now he grasped her arms and applied gentle pressure to turn her in his direction. Placing his thumb and forefinger beneath her chin, he angled her face upward so that she couldn't continue to avoid him.

"T.J. is my son? My flesh and blood?" His tone was deliberately calm, displaying nothing of the maelstrom of emotions churning through his gut.

"The one night that you and I—"

"We used protection," he reminded her and she nodded, bit her lower lip as he had seen her do so often when she was upset.

"We did, but it must not have worked. I found out I was pregnant right before I was supposed to marry Tim—"

"And you didn't tell him?" he said and ripped away from her, pacing across the room with a ground-eating stride or two before facing her once again.

Her brown eyes sparkled with indignation at his attack. "I could never mislead someone like that," she said, but then pulled back, obviously acknowledging that she had misled him. That he had a right to be angry and he definitely was angry. Probably more furious than he'd ever been before—except possibly on the day that he had learned Macy had decided to marry Tim.

Sucking in a rough breath, he walked back toward her, but stopped when he was about a step away. He didn't trust himself to get any closer at that moment. Fisting his hands tightly, he kept them at his sides, struggling for control.

"Why didn't you tell me?"

She shrugged and looked down once again before lifting her face. Her eyes glimmered with tears as she said, "Jericho was going on and on about how happy you were to join the Army. How you were looking forward to seeing the world and leaving Esperanza behind."

"And you assumed—"

"I didn't want to stop you and…you never called me again and Tim… He was a good man. I knew he would be a good father." A tear finally leaked out and trailed down her face, but she did nothing to swipe it away.

Nor did he. Instead, he took the final step to bring him close and leaned down until they were nearly nose-to-nose. "*I'm* a good man—"

"I know you are. You're a real hero. One who's made a difference to so many other people. Saved lives. That wouldn't have happened if you had stayed here…with me," she said and reached up, cradled the side of his face.

Her tender touch nearly undid him, but he couldn't leave it at that. "Did you love me? When you walked down the aisle—"

"I loved Tim with all my heart."

He had thought he was over the pain of losing her to another man, but the ache deep in the center of him told him otherwise. Her words were creating as much hurt now as her actions had eighteen years earlier.

But he couldn't retaliate and wound her, even if he was in agony with her admission.

He also couldn't let her continue to hide behind her love for Saint Tim.

Cradling her cheeks with both hands, he finally wiped away the trail of tears on her face with his thumb. Stroked the soft skin of her cheek and bent that final inch so that his lips were close to hers. He whispered, "You wanted me then and you want me now."

Then he kissed her like there was no tomorrow because he knew there might not be. As honor-bound as he felt to help Macy now that he knew T.J. was his son, he was also sure that he was not cut out for family or civilian life.

There was just too much uncertainty unlike the orderly military life that had worked so well for him, he told himself even as he kept on kissing Macy. Opening his mouth against hers over and over until it wasn't enough and he finally slipped his tongue within to taste the sweetness of her breath.

She responded to him willingly, going up on tiptoe to

continue the kiss. Pressing against him until he needed more. He slipped his hands beneath her buttocks and lifted her until her backside was on the edge of the counter and her legs were straddling him.

Macy shivered as the hard jut of his erection brushed the center of her, awakening a rush of desire that dragged a moan from her.

The sound penetrated the fog of want that had wrapped itself around them, tempering their kisses. Creating a short lull during which she managed to murmur a soft, "I'm sorry. I should have told you about T.J."

The reminder of her deception stilled his actions and he lifted his lips from hers, but remained close, his hands tangled in her hair. His body intimately pressed against her.

"Macy, I wish that things could be different, only—"

"Ma, I'm hungry," they heard loud and clear from T.J.'s bedroom upstairs.

The typical teen moment shattered the emotional angst and lust that had overtaken them.

Fisher released a rough sigh and stepped away while she called up to her son, "I'll be up with something in a minute."

She slipped off the counter and gestured to the oak kitchen table. "Will you stay for lunch?"

He nodded, but quickly added, "Let me help you with it."

She sensed that the hero in him intended to help her with more than lunch, much like she had asked. As much as she appreciated that he would do so, she also hoped that she wasn't making a mistake that would not only break her heart, but hurt her son.

When she acquiesced to his request, she quickly pulled out a can of condensed tomato soup from one cabinet and handed it to him. "Can you make this while I put together some sandwiches?"

"Can do," he said and she headed to the fridge for the fixings for lunch. She had some leftover roast beef that she could slice up for sandwiches and as she prepared them, she kept half an eye on Fisher as he made the soup.

He went into the fridge and removed a bottle of salsa and some shredded cheddar cheese. After opening the can and adding the water, he proceeded to put in a few heaping spoonfuls of the salsa to the soup. As she plated the sandwiches, he poured the steaming hot soup into bowls and topped them off with some of the shredded cheese.

Grabbing a tray from beneath the island counter, she prepped T.J.'s lunch, added a glass of milk to the tray and took it up to him.

The short nap he had taken seemed to have made a difference. He appeared more alert and not as pale as before and so it was with a lighter heart that she went back to the kitchen.

Fisher had set the table, laid out the soup and sandwiches for each of them along with fresh mugs of coffee.

"Thank you," she said and offered him a tired smile as she sat down beside him.

"You may not be thanking me when this is all over," he said and picked up half of his roast beef sandwich.

"Why's that?"

Fisher thoughtfully chewed the bite of sandwich before responding with, "Because if I'm going to help you, I intend to make sure that T.J. is being totally upfront with you, me and the sheriff."

She paused to consider him as he resumed eating and realized that he was in his military mode, where there were rules that needed to be followed and the failure to do so had consequences. She had tried to follow the same basic principles in raising her son, but too often since Tim's death, she had cut T.J. slack about the consequences part. In retrospect, she had done so to try and soften his father's loss, but had Tim been alive, he wouldn't have put up with T.J.'s behavior.

Fisher wouldn't either and that might be a good thing. "I agree that we need to get to the bottom of why T.J. isn't telling us what he saw today."

Fisher paused with his soup-filled spoon in mid-air, clearly surprised by her agreement. When he realized she was on board with him, he said, "And what's actually up with the missing girl. Sara, right?"

"Sara Engeleit," she confirmed and finally took a spoonful of the soup. The salsa and cheese had transformed the simple soup and her stomach growled noisily in appreciation.

"It's delicious," she said and quickly ate another spoonful.

"A bachelor's got to know how to take care of himself," Fisher said, but knew he had made a mistake when Macy's eyes darkened with sadness. Despite that, he had no doubt that it made sense to remind her of what he was and what he would continue to be once he was done helping her.

"Tell me about Sara," he said in an attempt to draw her attention to something besides their confusing and basically non-existent relationship.

With a shrug, she said, "Not much to tell. She came to the ranch about a week and a half ago. Right before T.J. and Joe started working at the Hopechest."

"Do you know where she's from?" After he asked the question, he took a bite of his sandwich.

Macy likewise took a bite, rolled her eyes upward as if

trying to gather all that she knew about the girl before responding. "She's sixteen and from Dallas, we believe. When she arrived at the ranch, she had some bruises on her arms and hands, but she seems to be from a family that's fairly well-off judging from her clothes and behavior."

"What about your boss? Does she know anything more?"

"Yesterday morning Jewel mentioned hiring a private investigator since Sara was missing. She was supposed to get a name from Joe Colton, but I haven't talked to her since then."

"Maybe after lunch—"

"I'll call her," she said and after that, the two of them quickly finished up the last of their soup and sandwiches.

While Fisher cleared off the table and tackled the dishes, she phoned Jewel to fill her in on all that had happened, beginning with the hit-and-run incident with T.J.

"Is he okay?" her friend asked, her concern evident in the tones of her voice.

"Bruised and banged up a little, but nothing serious luckily."

A heavy sigh filled the line. "I'm not liking this, Macy. There's just too much going on for it all not to be related."

"I agree, but without any more info—"

"Actually, Joe Colton was able to provide me some information about the man he believes to be Sara's dad—Howard Engeleit," Jewel said and relief flooded through Macy that they might finally have something to go on.

"Mr. Colton knows him?"

"When I mentioned Sara's last name, it rang a bell with Joe. Apparently Howard Engeleit had once worked with him. He says he didn't care for the man and that they'd had a falling out. He left Joe's company some time ago," Jewel recounted.

"Does he know where Howard is now?" she asked as

Fisher finished washing the dishes and stood there, drying his hands on a towel as he listened.

"Howard started his own company and made a good chunk of money. He and Joe see each other occasionally. The last that he had heard, Howard was in the middle of a nasty divorce battle, but Joe couldn't recall whether or not Howard had any children."

Although the information wasn't yet complete, she was relieved that at least now they might have something more to go on in their search to discover what was going on with her son and Sara. "Thanks for all the info. Fisher and I—"

"Fisher and you? Are you a team now?" Jewel said teasingly, unaware of just how problematic being together with Fisher was for her.

"We're going to check into some things and keep you posted. If you find out anything else, could you call me?" she responded, steering clear of any further discussion of her and Fisher.

"I understand, Macy. When you're ready to discuss it…"

"I'll let you know. Talk to you later," she said and hung up.

Fisher had walked back to the table and now he stood there, hands braced along the top rung of one of the kitchen chairs.

"You've got something to go on," he said.

"Something, but we need a little more. Seems like there's one sure way of finding out more about Howard Engeleit," she said, picked up her hands and mimicked that she was typing.

"The Net is bound to turn up something. Where's your computer?"

Chapter 14

The Internet search on Howard Engeleit immediately revealed hundreds of hits on the man.

As Macy skimmed through the various Web search results, it became apparent that Joe Colton wasn't kidding about Howard making himself money as a mover and shaker. There was account after account of Howard's business dealings, including some questionable ones. Much as Joe had said, Howard was in the midst of a difficult divorce but as luck would have it, the news articles mentioned a young daughter. Sara.

On one Dallas gossip page, there was even a picture of Howard, his wife Amanda and their daughter Sara. Howard's presence dominated the photo and Macy immediately got vibes from the submissive body posture of both his wife and daughter.

With Fisher sitting beside her and reading along, she gestured to the two women in the photo and pointed out how they seemed to be uneasy. "See their body posture and their eyes are downcast. Howard's clearly the one in control here."

Fisher nodded and agreed. "I've seen the same kind of body language on fresh recruits. He's definitely the one calling the shots."

"It may be more than that. Sara had bruises on her arms and hands when she first got to the ranch. If Howard was responsible, Sara might feel powerless to say anything about the abuse."

Fisher leaned back in his chair and rubbed his hand across his lips, thoughtful for a moment. "He's wealthy and connected, so who would believe her?"

She nodded emphatically. "Exactly. And if he's suing for custody of her—"

"He would have free rein to keep on abusing her." Fisher shook his head, sat up in the chair and clasped his hands together tightly. "It's sad that a father would do that to his child. That she feels there's no one there she can turn to."

"It's probably why she came to the ranch."

Fisher glanced up the stairs toward T.J.'s room. "Do you think he knows about the abuse? Is that why he's protecting her?"

She thought of T.J. and how much he was like the man who had raised him. Tim had been good-hearted and prone to helping others. But also, deep within her son were the genes from the man sitting beside her. A man of action. A hero. Combine the two and it was starting to make sense that T.J. was somehow involved with helping the young woman.

"I think that T.J. believes he's doing what's right for Sara, but the best thing would be to tell us what's happening so the authorities can handle this," she admitted.

He nodded, but then his gaze dropped down at his hands for a moment before he faced her. "There are times when a man has to make his own stand no matter what the rules say about what's right."

She heard him, but couldn't agree. Laying her hand on his tightly clasped ones, she said, "But he's not a man, Fisher. He's a boy. A scared and confused young boy."

Fisher eased his hands away from hers and pointed to the monitor. "You said that the deputy mentioned that Sara had been at a place up on the highway before she came to the ranch. We should print out that picture of her and check out that honky tonk. She might have run back there again."

She felt dismissed much as she suspected his men might feel when he gave them an order. She tried not to take it personally, telling herself that he was a man used to being in charge and making decisions.

But she was also used to being in control of her own life. Some might say she hadn't done a good job of it—heck, she even felt that way at times—but she had tried her best.

Her silence must have registered with him since he shifted his attention from the monitor and the prints he was making and back to her.

The strain on Macy's face was evident and Fisher struggled for a moment with a reason for it until it finally came. "Do you want to go that place on the highway or is there something else you think we should do?"

"I know you're used to taking control—"

"It's a hard habit to break," he freely admitted. In his life a delay in decision-making could cost someone their life, but he understood this wasn't the military.

"I didn't mean to order you around only...I feel like you and T.J. are my responsibility now." He paused as the strain on her face increased and sadness crept into her eyes. He wondered at it once again, although she was quick to make the reasons clear.

"Is that all we are? A responsibility?"

He mumbled a curse beneath his breath, regretting that his time alone and in the Army had seemingly cost him so many of his skills with women. Needing to reach her, both physically and emotionally, he cupped her cheek and tenderly ran his finger along the ridge of her cheekbone.

"I'm so not good at this, Macy," he confessed.

"This? As in—"

"Family life. Personal relationships. I don't know how to deal with the kinds of things you've had to handle. Difficult things like Tim's death and T.J.'s problems."

"I've done the best I could," she replied, defensiveness in every line of her body and the tight tone in her voice.

"You have and asking for my help isn't a bad thing…I don't think. But there's a lot I have to deal with also and I'm trying to do it the best that I can as well." He couldn't say it, but his reawakened feelings for Macy and the surprise announcement that he had a son were creating doubt within him. Doubt about the decisions he had made in his life. Doubt about the future he had thought to be fairly certain.

Now nothing seemed sure anymore except for the fact that he had to help Macy and T.J. His honor demanded it. He just hoped his heart would be intact when it was all over.

Macy nodded and after a shaky inhalation, her words came out on a rushed breath. "We'll do the best we can together for now."

Together for now. It seemed like the best thing they could hope for at that moment.

"Do you want to go to this honky tonk?" he asked again, trying for that togetherness.

The tension ebbed slowly from her body. "I think that's a good idea. I just want to check on T.J. first. Is that okay?"

"That sounds fine."

She laid her hand over his as it rested on her cheek, the action achingly tender and causing a funky tightening in his heart.

"Thank you for trying."

He bit back the words he had been about to say—that it was the least he could do. He had never believed in doing the least of anything in his whole life and Macy and T.J. certainly deserved more from him. Instead he said, "I will give it my all to make sure this comes out right."

A glimmer of a smile came to her face. "I'm certain you will."

Her trust in him moved him once again, choking his throat tight. Unable to say more for fear of what he might say, he nodded.

"I'm going to go check on T.J. and then we'll go, okay?"

"Okay," he managed to eke out and returned his attention to printing out larger pictures of Sara, both alone and with her parents.

He heard the tread of her steps going up the stairs and past the whir of the ink-jet printer, the soft and loving way she called T.J.'s name. A moment later, she descended the steps again and reentered the kitchen carrying the tray with the empty plates and glasses with T.J.'s lunch.

"He's sound asleep again. I left him a note that we were stepping out for a little while," she advised and went to the sink to clean the plates.

"That's good. It'll give us some time to visit this place and try to figure out where Sara may have gone." With a final *thunk-thunk,* the printer spit out the last sheet of paper with the photo of Sara.

He stood, picked up the papers, folded them neatly and tucked them into the pocket of his chambray shirt. Macy joined him just a second later.

"Are you ready to go?"

She nodded. "As ready as I'll ever be."

The Amarillo Rose sat on one of the smaller county roads, but one well-traveled by truckers avoiding the some-times more crowded state highways. Sitting smack dab in between Esperanza and another rural town, the location made it a great watering hole for the truckers who were headed from the Corpus Christi area to Lubbock or other northern cities.

The paint on the sprawling one story structure was a faded color which had probably once been yellow based on the name of the place and the slightly more colorful neon sign of a yellow rose close to the roadway. A couple of tractor trailers were parked off to the side of the building and a Chevy Silverado that was at least a decade old sat near the door.

As they walked by the truck, they noticed the name of a fish company painted on the door along with a Dallas address.

Macy took it to be a good sign.

She entered first, her eyes adjusting to the dimmer light. A small podium stood by the door and beyond that, a long bar to the left. In the center of the space were dozens of tables and chairs and to the far right, a small dance floor and bandstand.

Plastic bunting in red, white and blue emblazoned with

the name of a local beer hung from the ceilings. The walls were adorned with yet more ads and neon signs for an assortment of beers.

At the bar, a bartender was filling a glass with beer while a waitress laid out a plate for one of the three customers seated at the counter.

Fisher placed a hand at the small of her back and after a quick exchange of gazes, urged her toward the bar. She took a seat as did he and the bartender approached after setting the beer in front of one of the patrons. He slapped down paper coasters on the relatively clean surface of the bar.

"What can I get you folks?" He inclined his head in Macy's direction.

"An iced tea for me," she answered and Fisher immediately added, "And another for me."

The bartender quickly shifted away to get their orders and the waitress came to their side, held the menus before her as she said, "Can I get you folks some food? We've got a mean five alarm chili today as well as a to die for peach cobbler."

Fisher met her glance for only a second. "Peach cobbler for me. With vanilla ice cream if you've got it."

"We sure do, honey. What about you, ma'am. Same thing as your husband?" the waitress asked.

Macy was about to protest her mistake, but then thought better of it. If the waitress thought they were concerned parents searching for their daughter, she might be more inclined to help them. "I'll just have the cobbler, thanks."

The waitress walked away to fill their orders while the bartender came by with their drinks. "Here you go, folks. Is there anything else I can get you?"

Fisher pulled the photo of Sara from his pocket and as he

did so, she quickly spoke up. "My husband and I are looking for our daughter, Sara."

Fisher masked his surprise well, she thought, as he pushed forward the picture they had taken off the Internet.

"We think she might have come through here. Maybe a couple of weeks ago," Fisher said.

The bartender peered at the photo and then called out to one of the men sitting farther down the bar, "Maybe only… Hey, Billy Joe. Didn't you say that you gave a young girl a ride a few days ago?"

Billy Joe, a grizzled older man sporting a trucker's hat, slid off his stool and approached them. Leaning toward the picture on the bar, he placed his hands on his lips and tipped the hat back, exposing his Marine-buzzed salt and pepper hair.

"Yep. Picked her up just outside of Esperanza on…" The man rubbed the thick graying stubble on his cheeks as he tried to recollect. Finally, he said, "I think about two nights ago. She was on the road all by herself trying to get back to some ranch just outside of town."

"The Hopechest Ranch?" she asked and the old man nodded.

"I think that was the place. Dropped her off at the end of the driveway and she hightailed it up to the front door and went in."

"Your company's from Dallas, though, right. Do you do the drive from there regularly?" Fisher asked.

"I do. Funny you should mention that," the old man said, still rubbing at his cheeks. "When the young lady saw the name on the truck, she asked me if I was headed to Dallas. Seemed to me she didn't want to go back there if she could avoid it."

"Have any other strangers passed through here recently?" she asked, glancing back and forth between the bartender and truck driver. The waitress came over at that moment with their cobblers as the bartender said, "Have you seen any new faces around, Alice?"

A frown created a ridge above the older woman's eyebrows as she considered the question. "Just that salesman who said he was on his way to San Antonio. Didn't seem like much of a salesman to me."

"Why's that?" Fisher questioned.

"Got the most expensive thing on the menu. Didn't ask for a receipt and left a lousy tip," she said and wiggled her fingers to indicate that she wanted to see the photo.

After Fisher handed it over and she examined it, she said, "Don't remember the girl."

He pulled the other photo from his pocket and passed it to the waitress. "Was this the salesman?"

She glanced at it, but shook her head and placed the photo on the counter of the bar. "Don't recognize him."

"Me, neither," said the truck driver as did the bartender.

She exchanged a glance with Fisher, who handed the bartender the photo of Sara. "Do you think you could keep this just in case Sara comes by again? We can give you a phone number where you can call us."

"Sure." The bartender plucked a pen from inside his apron and jotted down the cell phone number that Macy provided.

Although they had ordered the desserts, she had no appetite thanks to the disappointment of discovering virtually nothing about Sara. The only worthwhile information they could pass to Jericho when he returned in a day or two would be the name of the company that the truck driver worked for and the license plate number. It wouldn't be all that much harder for Jericho to get the man's name based on that and their description of the truck driver. She didn't believe the older man had done anything, but Jericho could hopefully confirm that the man had no prior record.

Fisher bent close to her and whispered in her ear. "Do you want to go?"

"I'm not really very hungry," she admitted.

He brushed a kiss along her brow and laid his arm around her shoulders. "Let's go home then. Maybe T.J. will be able to tell us more once we tell him what we know about Sara's dad."

The tenderness of that caress chased away some of the disappointment. "Let's go home," she confirmed.

Chapter 15

They were on their way to Macy's, but it must have occurred to her that they would have to go past the Hopechest Ranch to reach her house.

She laid a hand on his arm as he drove the Jeep along the country road. "Do you mind if we drop by the ranch and speak to Jewel? I'd like to share what little we have and see if she maybe has some information for us."

"Not a problem." He slowed the Jeep as they neared the driveway for the ranch, then turned onto it and drove up to the front of the house.

After he had parked, he said, "Do you want me to go with you?"

"Of course. Together, right?"

Together for now, he thought, but couldn't disappoint. She had been too discouraged after their visit to the roadside canteen. Because of that, he nodded and followed her as she walked to the front door and entered, calling out Jewel's name as she did so.

A very pregnant woman—Mexican, young and pretty— was the first one to respond.

"Macy. Miss Jewel is in the library with Joe," the woman said.

"Is something wrong, Ana?"

Ana wrung her hands together and glanced toward the back of the house. "Joe said he had to talk to Miss Jewel. That he had something to tell her about Sara."

Macy placed her hand over her stomach and wavered on her feet. Fisher was immediately there, his hand at her shoulder to offer support and comfort.

"Let's go see if Jewel can talk to us," he said and squeezed her shoulder.

She reached up and placed her hand on his, seeking his solace and he offered it, easing his hand down so that she could grab hold of it.

Together they walked the few steps back to the library, a moderately sized room filled with books, a leather sofa and chairs as well as a small table where the children could read or study with some measure of quiet.

The door was ajar as they approached and Macy could hear the gentle tones of Jewel's voice as she spoke to Joe.

She knocked on the door, but no one responded. She was about to knock again when Jewel came to the entrance to the library.

"Macy. I'm so glad you're here." Her sharp-eyed gaze immediately went to Fisher behind her, down to where their hands were joined and then back up to her face.

"You have news?" Jewel asked.

"Not all that much unfortunately. And you?"

Jewel opened the door wide and held out her arm. "Why don't you come in. You need to hear what Joe just told me."

Her stomach did a little flip-flop, sensing the news would not be good. She tightened her hand on Fisher's.

They entered the room. Joe was seated on the maroon leather coach, but stood as he saw them. He nodded his head in greeting and said, "Mrs. Ward. Mr. Yates."

As anxious as she was, she couldn't muster the energy for niceties. "Your aunt tells us that you've got something we should hear."

The boy shifted from foot to foot and stuffed his hands in his pockets. He inhaled deeply and held it before finally speaking. "I saw Sara and T.J. together the afternoon before she disappeared. They were by themselves at the corral and Sara seemed upset."

"Upset with T.J.?" Fisher asked, but the boy quickly shook his head.

"I don't think so. It seemed like T.J. was trying to make her feel better. I think he has a crush on her," Joe said.

Jewel came up to stand by Joe and placed her arm around his shoulders. "Tell them what else you heard."

Joe fidgeted once again, clearly uneasy about what he would say and possibly, about betraying a friend's confidence. Macy understood that and so she tried to relieve that concern.

"I know you want to protect your friends, but if it's something that could get them hurt—"

"T.J. was telling Sara not to worry. That he would take her to a place where no one could find her."

"Was there someone Sara was afraid of? Someone who had found her here at the Hopechest?" Fisher asked.

"Maybe," he began and shrugged. "The other night—the night of the accident—another car started following us. Sara got worried and that's why T.J. was speeding, to get away from that car."

She recalled T.J.'s explanation that the other car had been challenging them, but this made a great deal more sense. If Sara's father had sent someone to try and find her, they might have spotted her in the car with the boys and decided to follow them to see where she might be.

"She was with you the night of the accident," Macy said, wanting to confirm her suspicions.

Joe exchanged a pained look with Jewel and nodded. "She was with us, but after we got into the accident, that car that had weirded us out was driving by. Before T.J. and I realized it, she had slipped out of T.J.'s car and somehow got back to the ranch without us."

Macy sensed something even more troublesome approached and at the thought of it, her knees began to shake. If Fisher hadn't already been gently guiding her toward one of the wing chairs, she would have sagged into one ignominiously.

"There's more, isn't there?"

Joe dropped his head until the only thing she could see was the tousled mass of his dark brown hair. He mumbled something, almost beneath his breath, but at Jewel's prodding, finally spoke up.

"I saw Sara getting into T.J.'s car the night before she disappeared. I'd heard some noises out by the one barn and went out to check. There wasn't anything by the barn, but on the way back, I saw a car in the distance and someone running to it."

"Are you sure, son? It was nighttime and you were quite a distance away," Fisher said.

Joe nodded and as he raised his blue-eyed gaze to them, it was filled with guilt. "I'm sorry, but it was T.J. and Sara. I saw their faces when T.J. opened the door and the lights came on."

She sighed and buried her head in her hands. If what Joe said was true—and she had no reason to doubt him—T.J. was headed for major trouble once the deputy found out. Before he did, she had to get to the bottom of what was really going on with her son.

Rising, she stepped up to Joe and her boss, her hands clasped tightly before her. "I know this is a lot to ask—"

"We're not supposed to speak to Deputy Rawlings until tomorrow and actually, I was hoping to wait until Jericho came back. He's due any day now, isn't he?" Jewel asked, her head cocked in Fisher's direction.

"Dad says he'll be back either tomorrow or the next day, although the next is more likely," Fisher replied. He laid his hand on her shoulder once again and said, "That gives us time to talk to T.J. and find out what's going on."

She nodded and embraced Jewel. "Thank you for understanding."

Jewel hugged her hard and brushed a lock of stray hair away from her face. "Call us as soon as you know anything. In the meantime, I'm going to speak to Clay Colton about those noises again. Find out if he can go out on the range to see if it's an injured animal."

"I'll call as soon as we have something." Turning, she took hold of Fisher's hand and they left the ranch house, jumped in the Jeep and raced home.

She knew something was wrong from the moment they pulled up into her driveway. There was something just too… quiet about the house. After she exited the Jeep, she immediately walked to the garage doors, stood on tiptoe and peered in through the glass windows.

T.J.'s GTO was gone.

Running to the front door, she threw it open and shouted his name.

When silence answered, she tore up the stairs, the house's old bones creaking from the force of her strides.

At T.J.'s door, she stared at his empty unmade bed.

He wasn't anywhere in the room.

Things had just gone from bad to worse.

He was getting slow in his old age, Fisher thought as he bounded up the stairs, chasing Macy after her mad dash from the garage and into the house.

He nearly barreled her over as she stood silently at T.J.'s door, her shoulders nearly heaving as she apparently struggled for control. He realized why as he stood behind her and peered over her shoulder into the room.

Her son...*their* son was gone.

Disappointment slammed into him as he thought of how T.J. had broken the rules of his punishment. He couldn't imagine how Macy felt, but he could see it in the lines of her body.

He stepped close and embraced her from behind, wrapping one arm across her waist while stroking her hair with his hand. "It'll be okay, Mace. We'll find him."

She sucked in a ragged breath while her body vibrated with tension. "Why would he do this? Why couldn't he talk to me?"

He remembered himself at T.J.'s age, all full of perceived male empowerment, but struggling with the confusing emotions about Macy, his mom and his life in Esperanza. Although he had been close to his father and brother, he hadn't been able to talk to them about all that he was feeling. He'd been too prideful, too perplexed and most of all, too angry.

"This isn't about anything you've done wrong, Mace. He's young and probably unsure of the situation he's gotten himself into with Sara. Women can do that to a man."

Another shuddering breath ripped through her body and transferred her pain to him and because he wanted to ease her anguish, he said, "I promise that this will work out. That we'll make this okay."

A big promise.

As she turned in his arms and wrapped hers around him, holding on to him as if for dear life, regret slammed into him that the promise he had just made might be one he would break because he didn't know how to make it okay. Had it been a mission with his men, he'd know the plan and what to do. Even if the plan got all messed up out in the field, he could find a way to make the mission work.

But this wasn't a mission and family things… They were far more complicated at times than a military mission and he feared he lacked the skills to be able to keep his promise.

Awkwardly he patted her on the back, held her as she cried out her frustration. He wasn't used to dealing with a woman's tears. Or a son's disobedience.

He couldn't tell her there was no crying in the military. Well, he could but it would be a lie because he had shed more than one tear over his men and their injuries. He also couldn't punish T.J. with a week in the brig for disobeying his mother.

In reality, he couldn't bring the kind of order he had in the Army to this family, but as Macy's tears finally subsided with a tiny hiccough that wrung his heart, he realized what he could do. He could bring her peace for a moment. Soothe her hurt and maybe make her smile.

As for T.J....

He needed a man's guidance to get him in line and he would try his best to help T.J. put his life in order. To fulfill his promise to make it okay before duty called for him to return to the Army.

Bending slightly, he cradled her face in his hands. Her cheeks were wet with her tears and slightly flushed. He wiped away the tears with his thumbs, brought his forehead to rest against hers once again and repeated his promise.

"It will be okay. *We* will make sure that everything is put to right."

As she nodded and gazed up at him, her brown eyes shimmering from her spent tears, he realized she believed in that promise. Believed in him.

His heart constricted again at the trust she had in him and he vowed to do his best not to disappoint her which meant that as difficult as it might be, they had to decide what to do about T.J.

Chapter 16

An open bottle of wine sat on the kitchen counter and he poured them each a small glass before making them a quick dinner.

Macy had protested, saying she wasn't hungry, but he had insisted. She needed to keep her strength up so that they would be ready to figure out what T.J. was doing and where he might have taken Sara, since both of them now had no doubt that he knew where the girl was.

Between the trip to the Amarillo Rose and the stop at the ranch, it was already dusk. T.J. had likely been gone for hours and what made the most sense was for them to refuel, get some rest and prepare to find T.J. the next day.

He also insisted on Macy helping him, hoping that the simple chores would help take her mind off things. As they worked together in the kitchen, he intentionally kept the talk away from T.J., wanting Macy to relax. If she felt more at ease, it might prompt some idea of where T.J. might have hidden Sara.

While Macy chopped onions and red peppers for the omelets, Fisher took out the eggs and found some bread to toast.

"There's only six eggs," he said, glancing down at the plastic egg tray from the refrigerator.

"There's only two of us," Macy replied with surprise.

"A man's got to get his protein," he said with a smile and rummaged through her fridge until he found a ham steak. Taking it out, he walked with it to the island counter where she was working and laid it before her.

"If the veggies are ready—"

"They are," she said and handed him the cutting board with the chopped peppers and onions. She grabbed another so she could cut up the ham.

"I'll get them cooking up," he said and little by little, with the two of them working side by side, the omelet and toast took shape.

Within less than half an hour, they were seated at the table, eating a delicious omelet. Silent as they finished the simple meal and sipped the last of the wine in the bottle. After, they cleared the table and cleaned the dishes together at the sink.

By the time they had finished, Macy was obviously more in control. More relaxed and truthfully, so was he. Being beside her…

It made him imagine what it would be like to have a family of his own. To do everyday things together like they had tonight. Simple things which somehow brought a peace to his heart that he hadn't experienced in some time.

She walked him to the door, but then they both stood there,

awkward. Uncertain. Lingering at the door, heads hanging downward. He wondered if she was as reluctant as he about all that had happened that day. About leaving her, although he was hesitant to admit that.

"Fisher," she said, her voice rising in question although she didn't pick up her head.

He bent a little, trying to see her face, but couldn't in the dim light of the bulb at the front door. He placed his thumb and forefinger beneath her chin and gently tipped it upward so that he could see her face.

"Macy?"

She kept her eyes downcast as she said, "I don't want to be alone tonight. Would you stay?"

Stay. With her?

It tightened his gut to imagine being with her. Lying beside her and yet…

She was vulnerable and he was…decidedly too puzzled about what she made him feel. Regardless of all that, as she finally tipped her eyes up shyly and the need there slammed into him, he realized he couldn't deny her request.

"I'll stay."

As they walked back into her home, he finally took the time to appreciate her house's simplicity. No fripperies or excessive feminine touches. He wondered if she had kept this home simple and feminine-free for Tim and T.J. If it was the kind of house she wanted or one she had settled for because of the men in her life.

Was this the kind of house they would have shared if things had been different or if she would have taken the time to stamp their home with her unique personality.

As she opened the door to her bedroom, he finally saw traces of her.

He knew little about design, so the best he could do was call it feminine. Lacey things adorned the rich mahogany furniture in the room. Floral curtains were at the two windows and a bedspread with a similar pattern of roses covered a queen-sized bed. To the far right of the bed sat a big soft chair and ottoman in a floral chintz pattern. A romance novel sat on the ottoman. The cover was up with the open pages facing the ottoman, marking the spot where she had stopped reading.

Macy paused in the middle of the room and gestured to a door at the other end. "The bathroom's in there in case you need to…you know."

He didn't need to do anything, but decided to give her a moment to collect herself. With a courteous nod, he went to the bathroom and shut the door behind him.

The decor of the bathroom was even more feminine. Lace decorated the one window and the light rose-colored towels were adorned with beige lace. A painted wrought-iron stand by the bathtub was fanciful as was another by the window which held an assortment of African violets blooming in shades of purple and pink.

He smiled at the flowers, which added so much life to the space, and walked over to touch the velvety surface of one bloom. Soft and lush. Like Macy's skin.

Wrong, wrong, wrong, he reminded himself. He needed to be in control if he was going to survive the night.

He walked to the pedestal sink, turned on the cold water and splashed his face with it over and over again until he had restored control.

Drying his face and hands with one of the very feminine towels, he then folded it neatly and laid it on the rack to dry.

When he walked back into her bedroom, her door was closed and the room was dimly lit by one small lamp on a nightstand by the bed. Macy was on top of the covers, fully clothed, her back turned toward the bathroom.

He wrung his hands nervously, then wiped them up and down on his jeans before taking a stutter step toward the bed.

She turned at the sound he made, leaned back on one hand as he approached. Her brown-eyed gaze looked him up and down, hesitant but hungry as he stopped at the edge of the bed.

"Are you sure?" he asked.

"I don't want to be alone tonight. I haven't been alone in this house since…"

"Tim died?"

Shaking her head vehemently, she said, "I bought this house and everything in it a couple of years after Tim died. T.J. and I…we needed a change. There were just too many sad memories at the old place."

Relief washed over him then. Relief that he wouldn't be lying in another man's bed. Beside another man's memories.

He sat on the edge of the bed and pulled off his boots. Tossed them aside and they landed with a thud on the polished hard wood floor.

Facing her, he copied her pose, leaning back on one hand as he considered her. "It must have been hard for you."

She lay down on her back and nodded. "I didn't want to believe it at first—that Tim was really going to die. Since we found out that he…"

She shuddered and closed her eyes before shifting to grab

the crocheted throw at the foot of the bed. She pulled it up around her, as if she was cold.

It tugged at him with the vulnerability it exposed and he shifted quickly, moving to her side and embracing her. Bringing her to rest beside him as he stroked his hand up and down her side, trying to soothe her.

"I know I said I was sorry at his funeral, but—"

She slipped her hand over his mouth. "Can we talk about something else?"

He frowned, confused until she said, "Could we talk about you? Why you chose the Army?"

He wanted to say "Because of you" but bit the words back. He had already been considering the Army before what had happened with her. What had happened with her had only cemented the decision he had already been about to make.

"My dad did a great job of giving Jericho and me stability after Mom left and I needed that after high school. Community college just wasn't doing it for me. I needed more."

"And the Army gave you that?" She cradled his cheek and stroked her thumb across the roughness of his afternoon beard.

He nodded, but it seemed to not be enough for her.

"Did you ever miss Esperanza while you were gone?"

He should have lied. It would have made things that much easier, but he was a man of honor and couldn't lie to her.

"I missed home more than I thought I would."

Macy told herself not to read anything into his words. "Jericho and your dad miss you a lot. They worry about you. So do a lot of people in town—you're our hero."

He smiled tightly, clearly uncomfortable with the praise. "I'm just doing my job."

"A job that could get you killed." She shifted her hand

down to rest on the hard muscles of his chest. Beneath her palm his heart beat strongly. Steadily, much like the man beside her.

He covered her hand with his, his palm rough on the back of hers. The thin white line of a scar marred one knuckle and another larger one was close to his wrist. The hand of a warrior.

"Almost more than anything, I want you to be safe and to be happy," she said, finally admitting to what had been in her heart for far too long.

"Almost more? Can I guess that what you want even more is to see T.J. safe and happy," he questioned, tenderly rubbing his hand back and forth against hers.

"Definitely."

He slipped his hand from hers and slid it into the short waves of her hair, softly cupping her head. "And what about you?"

"Me?" she asked, slightly befuddled until she met his brilliant green-eyed gaze and his meaning was clear. "What do I want?" she asked, just to be sure.

"Yes, what do you want for yourself?" he said, leaving no room for doubt about the answer he expected from her.

What did she want that was only for herself? she wondered, but then the answer came too swiftly to be denied any longer.

"I want you."

Chapter 17

A tremor rocked through the hand in her hair and beside her his body tensed.

"Macy," he said, his tone low and tinged with an odd combination of exasperation and need. He rolled onto his back, breaking contact with her.

She raised herself up on one elbow. "You were right when you said that I wanted you back in high school and that I want you now, but you know what else?"

He looked away, unable to meet her probing gaze as he asked, "What?"

"Want without love is empty. That's what I realized back in high school. That's why I married Tim," she finally confessed, thinking that he deserved a complete explanation after so many years.

The pain in his heart was almost more than he could bear

and so strong that he wanted to lash out at her. Before he could control himself, he had flipped and pinned her to the mattress, his body holding her down while he held her hands above her head.

"You never even gave me a chance to prove to you it was more," he said, his breath ragged in his chest from his distress.

"No, I didn't and that was wrong. I should have given you a chance, especially when I found out I was pregnant with T.J., only…"

"Only what, damn it! I deserve an answer as to why you kept my son from me for his entire life," he barked out.

"I was afraid of what I felt for you. I was afraid that if I gave you my heart, you'd break it when you left." Tears shimmered in her eyes, but she battled them back, biting her lower lip in a gesture that was all too telling and all too tempting.

He slowly loosened his grip on her hands and bent his head, bringing his lips to a hair's breadth from hers. "Maybe if you had asked, I wouldn't have left," he said and then closed the distance between them and kissed her. Put all of his heart and soul and eighteen years of frustration into showing her just what might have been between them.

The shock of his kiss, filled with such need and yearning, overcame any doubts Macy might have had about whether it was right to explore this. She opened her mouth to his and pressed her body upward, meeting the hardness of his muscled physique. The short strands of his dark hair were soft against her hands as she held his head to her, urging him on.

Over and over they kissed until they were both trembling. Until it wasn't enough and she lifted her hips against the press of his erection, so full and hard against her belly.

She shuddered and between her legs, her muscles clenched

on the emptiness there, but she reminded herself of her earlier words to him. About how empty want was without love.

She had no doubt she cared for him. About him. She had no doubt she could be falling in love with him. With his strength and goodness.

But she also knew that if that love was to grow true and strong, taking this any further tonight would be wrong. Fisher must have sensed it as well since he gave her one last kiss before slowly pulling away.

"I'm willing to wait until you're ready, Macy," he said, brushing away a tousled lock of her hair.

She nodded, but had to ask him. "What happens then, Fisher?"

Fisher wished he knew what to tell her. He wished he knew whether she ever would be ready for a relationship with him or whether he could commit to her if she was. Commit to having a wife and family after so many years in the military.

"I'm not sure," he confessed.

She faced away from him as she said, "Jericho said you might not sign up for another tour of duty. That you might teach instead."

Damn his brother for being such a busybody, he thought. Hadn't Jericho ever heard the old saying that loose lips sink ships?

"I've been offered a teaching post at West Point."

"And had you given any thought to it?" she asked, turning toward him once again, the resoluteness in her brown-eyed gaze drilling into him, daring him to lie to her, but he couldn't.

"I had given it some thought," he admitted and that seemed to be enough for her for the moment.

"I think it's time we got some rest," she said and flipped onto her side.

He nestled against her, his front to her back, spooned as close as he could be, and dropped his arm to rest across her waist while pillowing his head on his other arm.

"Good night, Mace."

"Good night, Fisher," she said and laid her arm over his.

For long moments he lay there, listening to her breathe until the rhythm of it deepened and lengthened, confirming to him that she slept. Even then he clung onto wakefulness, trying to experience this peaceful interlude. Wondering how it might be if she lay beside him every night. What it would be like to sample the passion he had experienced but for a brief moment earlier that night.

As he drifted off, the taste of her on his lips and the memory of her pressed close, it occurred to him that maybe family life might not be such a bad thing.

That maybe it was worth giving that teaching position more than just a thought.

He awoke to the smell of fresh coffee and Macy. Her scent lingered on the sheets long after she had left the bed.

He took his time to snuggle her pillow close and savor that rose-filled scent. Maybe even memorize for the future if it turned out to be that his nights were meant to be without her.

Realizing he couldn't dawdle for long, however, he rose and went to the bathroom where he relieved himself and after, washed his face and hands. Put a little of her toothpaste on his finger and scrubbed his mouth out the best he could.

Thankfully, it took just his fingers to rake smooth the short strands of his hair and then he was on his way downstairs and to the kitchen, where Macy was standing at the counter, fork-splitting some English muffins.

"Good morning," he said and came up behind her, dropped a quick kiss on the side of her face.

"Mornin', Fisher. I walked over to the corner store and got some more eggs. Figured I'd make us a bite to eat while we decided what to do today."

"Let me help," he said, grabbed the muffins and brought them to the toaster while Macy cracked the eggs.

After he popped the muffins into the toaster oven and got it cranking, he leaned back against the counter and asked, "Have you given any thought to where T.J. might have taken Sara?"

She shook her head as she scrambled the eggs and said, "I've been thinking about that ever since yesterday. Joe said T.J. thought no one would find her there…"

Her voice trailed off and she stopped whipping. She put down the fork and bowl and said, "We used to go hiking and camping about thirty miles from here in the Texas hill country."

Wiping her hands on her apron, she headed toward a side door in the kitchen and he followed.

The door opened into the two-car garage which had a recessed area on one side. Shelves and a large plastic storage bin were tucked into the recess and Macy immediately went to the storage bin and pulled up the top.

"The camping equipment and knapsacks are gone. T.J. must have taken them and if he did that…I bet that's where he took her. We used to go up in the hills and camp. We even found a cave one time."

"Was the cave big enough for someone to hide in or stay for any length of time?" he asked.

"Definitely. We slept there one night when it was raining,"

she said with a quick bob of her head. "T.J. and his dad used to go there often until… I only went a few times, though. Hiking and camping were not my thing."

"Do you think you could take us there? Find the trail that T.J. would be most likely to use to get to the cave?"

"I think so. It's been a while, but I'm good at remembering places. We'll need some supplies—"

"I've got camping gear back at Dad's house and we can stop by the feed and supply to pick up some MREs."

"MREs?" she questioned, clearly unfamiliar with the term.

"Ready to eat meals. Dad has everything we need in his camping section," he explained.

"I'll get changed and pack some warmer clothes. It can get cold in the hills."

"And they're predicting heavy rains. I hope T.J. knows enough to stay to the high ground and away from those arroyos. They can be dangerous if there's a flash flood."

Macy paled a little, but kept her cool. "I hope he knows that as well. I'll be down in a few minutes."

"I'll finish cooking breakfast. The food will help us to be prepared for a long day."

As Macy walked back into the kitchen and he went about finishing the meal, he only hoped that by the end of the day, they would have a better idea of where T.J. and Sara might be.

Fisher had called Buck Yates ahead of time and his dad had a few days worth of rations as well as some maps of the area ready for them when they arrived at his feed and supply store on the outskirts of town. Combined with the camping equipment that Fisher had picked up at his dad's house, they would be well-prepared for a trip into the hill country.

As Buck helped them stow supplies in their knapsacks, Fisher asked, "Is Jericho still due home tomorrow?"

Buck nodded. "As far as I know he is."

Fisher shot a look at her and said, "Tell him that we think T.J.'s helping Sara and that they're hiding up in the state park. We'll check in with the park ranger when we get there, but Jericho should try and reach me on the cell phone as soon as he can."

When their bags were packed, they tossed them into the back of Fisher's Jeep, climbed in and started the ride to the state park. It was about thirty miles away in the hill country and easily reached along a small interstate.

The weather station had predicted torrential rains for that afternoon. Macy hoped that they could reach the park and pick up T.J.'s trail before the rains came and obliterated any sign of him and Sara.

The weather forecast was on her mind during the entire ride along with concerns about what would happen if Deputy Rawlings decided to come by the house to question T.J. Would he assume the worst if he found them all gone? If he did, would he issue an all points bulletin for T.J. as if he were a fugitive?

At her prolonged silence during the ride, Fisher glanced at her out of the corner of his eye. "Don't worry. We'll find them before there's any more problems," he reassured her.

"If Deputy Rawlings—"

"Jericho will be home soon enough and I think Rawlings is smart enough to know that Jericho would be less than pleased with the kind of grief he's already given you. He's not going to escalate this."

She shook her head, recalling the dour look on the deputy's handsome face when she had gone to pick up T.J. "He seemed pretty determined to me."

"Focus on what we'll do once we get to the park. Which trail we'll take and where T.J. might have hidden Sara," he urged and she did, forcing herself to remember the two or three trips she had taken with Tim and T.J. up into the hills. Trusting that between that and Fisher's military expertise in tracking, they could find where T.J. and Sara might have gone.

Hoping that whoever it was that had tried to run down T.J. or had been asking questions back at the honky tonk would not already be on the teen's trail.

Chapter 18

When Fisher pulled into the main lot of the state park, her heart skipped a beat.

Stationed at the farthest corner, beneath some thick oaks, was T.J.'s GTO. She pointed at it and Fisher drove to the car and parked beside it. As she stood beneath the canopy of the oaks, she realized why he had chosen the spot. It would be difficult for anyone searching from above to spot the car.

Fisher kneeled by the driver's side door, observing some impressions in the gravel by the car. He tracked the impressions to a dirt path besides the gnarly pines surrounding the parking lot. "The footprints lead from the car to here, but there's only one set that I can see."

"From last night when he came back to where he'd hidden Sara," she said.

He nodded, lifted his hand and pointed to the small ranger

station about thirty feet away on the opposite side of the lot. "Why don't you stay here while I talk to the ranger?"

If someone was chasing the teens, they might also have a picture of her and be showing it around. Better she lay low as well, she thought and eased back into the Jeep to wait for Fisher's return.

Nearly half an hour went by as she sat there, tapping her foot and fidgeting with her cell phone. She was on the verge of calling Fisher when she saw him via the rearview mirror, exiting the ranger station. He had a piece of paper in his hand which he glanced at once or twice as he came closer.

When he reached the car, he eased back in and laid out the paper—a map of the park areas—in the space between the two seats. "The ranger says there's at least three trails into the hills. One of them starts right here where T.J. parked."

He pointed to a spot on the map and she leaned over, followed the meandering uphill path of the trail on the paper until it arrived at an overlook.

She remembered such a spot at which she, Tim and T.J. had stopped on at least two of their hikes. Thinking back on it, the scenic hillside site had taken them nearly three hours to reach and she mentioned that to Fisher.

He examined the map and said, "Assuming you were only walking about two miles an hour, this overlook would be about six miles away so it seems as if this might be the trail T.J. would take since he was familiar with it."

Trailing her finger along the path, she stopped and circled one area on the map. "The rock face around here had a lot of openings. That's where we found a cave that one time and stayed inside overnight."

"Could be where T.J. stashed Sara," he said and then his

mouth tightened to a grim line as he jabbed at another spot on the map. "This is a bridge over an arroyo. Let's hope that it's more than a foot bridge and that they have the sense to stay away from it if the rains are as bad as they say they'll be."

Her stomach turned at the thought of how bad a flash flood could be high up in the hills. The water would come churning down the arroyos, sometimes ripping up small bushes and trees. Cascading with powerful roughness against anything in their path. Anyone caught up in the way of the raging waters faced serious injury or death.

"He'll know better," she said, but it was almost as if she was trying to convince herself.

"Are you ready to go? If we're lucky the rains will hold out until we've got a solid grasp on where T.J. was headed."

"I'm ready," she said. As she eased on the knapsack and adjusted its weight on her shoulders, she worried about why Sara had run away and why T.J. would have found it necessary to hide the young girl.

But then she remembered the bruises on Sara's arms when she had arrived at the ranch and T.J.'s comments about the driver who had challenged him a few nights ago. The teens had clearly been afraid of whoever was responsible for both.

Because of that, she hoped she and Fisher would find the teens before anyone else did.

Although heavy rains were expected later that day, it had been at least a week since it had rained and the ground was hard and dusty. Despite that, Fisher was able to track the impressions in the gravel by T.J.'s car to a distinctive set of sneaker treads on the dirt path leading to the trail.

"What size shoe does T.J. wear?" he asked.

"A thirteen," she responded and stood by him as he kneeled to examine the footprints.

"That's about the size of this shoe which confirms that T.J. probably went up this trail."

He rose and adjusted the straps on the knapsack, making sure they were tight so that the pack would not shift as they headed up the trail. From the trunk, he removed a rifle, eased the strap over his head and settled the weapon securely beside the pack on his back. Then he faced Macy, reached for her straps, but paused by the bindings on her knapsack.

"May I?" he asked.

She nodded and he quickly adjusted her pack to keep it from shifting and then gestured to the trail. "I'll lead the way. If I'm going too fast—"

"Believe me I'll let you know."

He smiled, ripped out a baseball cap from his back pocket and plopped it on her head. "Put this on. There'll be glare on the footpath and once it starts raining, it'll keep you dry."

"Thanks."

He grabbed his cowboy hat from the backseat of the Jeep and also put on a pair of polarized sunglasses which would help cut down on the glare. Taking the point, he focused on the sneaker tread pattern and followed it up the trail.

T.J. had not tried to hide his tracks. The footprints were clearly visible along the path. He had been in a hurry, however, judging from the wide distance between his steps. If he recalled T.J.'s height correctly, the space between the footprints indicated that he had been almost jogging up the trail.

If Macy hadn't been with him, he would have done the same, eager as he was to find the teens and put to right what was happening so Macy could have some peace of mind. But she was with him and so he kept his pace reasonable, his mind focused on tracking T.J., but also aware of how she was doing as she followed behind him.

About a mile up the path, T.J.'s stride began to shorten and about a quarter of a mile after that, they became the length of a normal walking step. He paused then and perused the path ahead of them as well as the open country all around.

Pines and oaks dotted the rolling hillsides. In between the stands of the trees were patches of grass and larger meadows which in the springtime would be awash with the colors of Texas wildflowers. Even now there were spots of bright color from some of the later blooming plants and stretches of prickly pear cactus. Up ahead of them, the trail wound through stands of trees before a limestone rock face rose up to the left, leading to the overlook Macy had identified on the map.

"It's beautiful, isn't it?" she asked as she stood beside him.

"It is," he said and pointed to a herd of fallow deer feeding on grass in one distant meadow, their almost white coats bright against the dull brown of the parched grasses.

Macy leaned against him and took hold of his hand as she witnessed the sight. "I wish that one day…"

He didn't need her to finish. He knew what she wished and inside of him, something had been slowly taking root since last night. Something that said maybe what they both wished wasn't so far apart.

Looking up the trail, he said, "You mentioned a cave?"

She nodded. "There's quite a few of them up ahead, but I think the biggest one is quite a ways up. Probably past the overlook and closer to the bridge."

Once again concern rose in him as he cast his gaze upward at the thickening clouds above. Inhaling deeply, he could smell the coming rain and hoped the forecasters were wrong about the force of the storm.

"Let's get going. The rain will be here soon," he said and they once again set off, following T.J.'s sneaker prints in the dust of the trail.

They had been on the winding path for another half an hour when the first fat raindrop plopped on the brim of his cowboy hat. He quickly removed two large rain ponchos from one of the pouches on his pack and helped Macy ease hers on over the backpack. Then he slipped on his own as the drops grew more frequent and quite heavy in a matter of seconds.

There was little shelter on the trail as they continued upward, just an occasional stand of oaks here and there, but they couldn't pause for any delayed shelter under the trees. The impressions of T.J.'s sneakers vanished quickly beneath the onslaught of the rain. The trail in front of them became a difficult morass of mud.

As they struggled ever onward, he kept his eyes trained on the areas around the trail to make sure T.J. had not detoured off the path. There wasn't any sign that he had deviated from continuing up the trail. If anything, up ahead he found an impression protected by a thick oak beside the trail. Bending down, he examined the footprint more closely just to make sure. It was T.J.'s.

Beneath the canopy of the oak, he offered Macy a drink and short respite from the mud and pounding rains they had been battling for nearly an hour.

She took a deep draw from the canteen and pulled off her baseball cap to wipe away a line of sweat from her forehead. "We're not even halfway to the overlook."

No, they weren't, he thought. He cradled her cheek and

said, "Don't worry. If we're moving this slowly, so is T.J. He won't get that much farther ahead. For all we know, he's taken refuge in one of the caves to wait out the storm."

Macy considered his words and prayed they were true. That would give them a chance to catch up to her son and Sara.

She dragged her hand across the back of her neck. She had tucked her hair up into a ponytail to try and stay cool, but with the rain the ponytail was dripping wet. Beneath the plastic of the rain poncho and heavy backpack it was hot, although once the sun went down, the temperature would cool quickly.

She glanced at Fisher who seemed as fresh as he had when they had first started the trek. Of course he would. As a soldier he was used to exercises like this. It was why he had taken the bulk of the supplies in his pack. She appreciated it since even the lighter weight in hers began to feel like a ton of rocks.

"How much farther will we go today?" she asked although she was determined to follow Fisher even if she had to crawl up the trail.

"Depends on how bad the footing becomes and how quickly it gets dark. We can't risk losing our balance once we're higher up on the trail."

She eased the baseball cap back on, pulling her dripping wet ponytail through the hole in the back. "I'm ready to go."

He smiled and tenderly passed his fingers down the side of her face. "I know you are."

Turning, Fisher once again set off up the trail, but as they cleared the protection of the oak, the rain pounded them once again. Beneath their feet, the ground was even more unsteady and their boots sank into the mud, making each step that much harder. At one point she slipped and fell to one knee. The cold of the rainwater soaked through the fabric of her jeans and she prayed T.J. had been sensible enough to take shelter from the storm.

As she struggled to rise in the muck, Fisher was there to help her up.

She took hold of his hand, but he didn't release it as they continued onward, slipping and sliding. Pressing ever onward until dusk came and darkness threatened. By that point, they were beside the limestone rock formations that held an assortment of crevices and breaks.

Fisher stopped at one, examining the size of the opening which was big enough for someone to slip through.

He turned to her and as he removed his pack, he said, "I'm going to check inside."

Leaving his pack propped up against the face of the limestone hillside, he easily sidestepped into the opening and exited quickly into a small cave. Clearly, someone had stayed inside. The cold remains of a firepit were in the center of the area and a small pile of tinder and wood sat along the wall.

He could barely stand upright, but there was enough space for a few people to comfortably sit or sleep. He snared a small penlight from his belt loop and flashed it along the edges of the cave. The exterior wall was fairly straight and toward the back of the cave another opening led deeper into the rock hillside. Stalactites had formed near that opening from beyond the sounds of dripping water echoed from deep within the cave.

Although the cave smelled damp, there appeared to be fresh air flowing through it, which would explain how they could build the fire within the small space. As he turned his penlight on the dirt floor of the cave, T.J.'s easily identifiable sneaker tread was visible in several spots along with a much smaller footprint.

T.J. and Sara had been there recently. Maybe last night, he hoped, thinking that if the two teens were up ahead they were also finding a dry place to spend the night. If he and Macy got an early start in the morning, they might be able to make up some ground on the teens.

He eased back out through the opening to where Macy stood huddled against the rock face, the rain pounding against her.

"T.J. and Sara were here recently. We can stay in the cave tonight."

Stepping beside her, he helped her slip off her pack and then led her through the opening before heading back out to bring in his own supplies.

Inside the cave, he gestured to the firepit. "Think that you can get a fire going?"

She pulled off her baseball cap and then her poncho, setting them by the entrance to the cave opening to dry. "My Girl Scout skills are a little rusty, but I think I can manage," she said, reached into her pocket and pulled out a small package which she wiggled in the air. "Your dad handed me some waterproof matches on the way out of his store."

He grinned and nodded. "There may be some deadfall just off the trail. It'll be wet, but should still get dry if we get a good fire going. There's some tinder and a small supply of wood just over there," he said and motioned to the far side of the cave wall.

He had left his pack and the rifle by the entrance of the cave as well and stopped to remove a small hatchet from the main storage area on the pack. Exiting the cave, he carefully eased down a side of the trail that had some small brush, saplings and luckily, the deadfall from an oak tree. With a few sharp strokes, he chopped away some larger branches which he carried back up to the cave before returning once again to gather some more wood.

When he had a good enough pile, he returned to the cave, set the hatchet by his pack and slipped off his dripping poncho and cowboy hat. His boots were soaked as well and so he took them off and placed them besides Macy's.

Turning, he realized she had a nice fire going. The smoke from the fire was being drawn back toward the interior of the cave. He suspected there was a break somewhere allowing the air to vent. Macy had also laid out a tarp on the cave floor and had their sleeping bags ready for later use. A cooking frame was set over the fire and she heated water in a small kettle beside another pot where something was steaming flavorfully.

"Smells great," he said as he placed the damp wood close to the fire to dry.

"Thank your dad for the prepackaged stew." She stirred the mixture in the pot before reaching beside her and grabbing a plastic bag. "We've got some biscuits I'll heat up as well."

"Do you mind?" he said and motioned to his wet jeans.

Macy gulped as she imagined what lay beneath the faded denim, but it made sense. She had planned to remove her own wet jeans as well once the meal was closer to done.

"Go ahead." She kept her eyes trained on the stew and once it bubbled, she tore open the package with the biscuits and laid them on the grate of the cooking frame to heat.

Before she knew it, Fisher was kneeling beside her, his sleeping bag wrapped around his hips.

"Why don't you get out of your wet things while I finish this up?"

She handed him the spoon for the stew and stepped away only long enough to peel off her damp pants and set them on top of her pack to dry. As he had done, she wrapped her sleeping bag around her waist and returned to sit by the fire.

Fisher gingerly flipped over the four biscuits with his fingers and he shot a quick glance at her. "Would you rather have tea or coffee?"

"Coffee would be great." After he had sprinkled grounds in the pot with the boiling water, she picked up the two divided plates she had removed from his backpack, held them out to him.

He snared the biscuits from the grate and placed them on the plates, then quickly spooned up the stew into one of the sections of the dish. As one they shifted away from the fire and sat, using the cutlery that came with the mess kits to eat.

Hunger took control and it was quiet as they both savored the meal. The heat of the fire helped chase away the damp and chill of the rain.

Macy watched as Fisher sopped up the stew sauce with the last of his biscuit and took pity on him, handing him her second biscuit.

"Are you sure?" he asked even as he was reaching for it.

"I'm full," she said and she was. The stew and first biscuit had been surprisingly filling. She grabbed a pot holder and picked up the coffeepot, swirled the liquid and grounds around before setting it back down on the grate to continue brewing.

While she did that, Fisher rose and removed a large thick plastic bag from his pack and placed the dirty dishes inside. "We'll wash them up later."

She nodded, grabbed the two mugs she had put by the fire earlier and poured them both steaming cups of coffee. She opened a plastic bag which contained dry creamers and sweeteners. After they had fixed their coffees, they sat and quietly sipped them.

The sound of the rain coming down continued outside and Macy grimaced. "Do you think it will let up soon?"

He blew on his cup of coffee and took a sip before answering. Shaking his head, he said, "Weatherman said the storm front would be with us until tomorrow night, but it shouldn't be as heavy during the day tomorrow."

Macy cradled the hot tin mug in her hands, enjoying the warmth of it more than the coffee within. When she finally took a sip, the coffee was strong and sweet. She peered over the edge of the mug to where Fisher sat, drinking his coffee and adding some wood to the fire.

The wood was still damp and as it heated; it began to snap and pop. Hissed as steam escaped from the log.

The heat grew pleasantly in the intimate space of the cave and she unzipped the sweatshirt she had put on, allowed the heat of the fire to soak in. But her growing comfort made her guiltily think about the kids and how they might not be as restful.

"Do you think T.J. and Sara—"

"They were in this cave. Probably last night. I'm sure they took shelter again today."

His words reassured her, until it occurred to her that she would once again be sleeping beside him. Sharing intimate space and given last night's talk, trusted feelings.

A scary and exhilarating realization.

Chapter 19

As he looked up from where he had been poking at the fire, trying to get it banked for the night, he didn't fail to notice the battling emotions on her face. He could even understand.

He would be sleeping beside her tonight. Again.

It scared him. Each time that he was beside her made it harder to think about leaving. And it terrified him to think about what would happen if he released the control he had exerted last night and finally explored his feelings for her.

Which brought an unwelcome tightening to his gut which he had to tamp down like the fire he was so diligently managing.

Yanking his attention back to the flames, he said, "Do you want any more coffee? I'm going to go clean the mess kits."

"I'll help—"

"No," he said more forcefully than he had intended. Repeating it softly, he said, "No, just stay warm and get comfortable. I think Dad packed some inflatable pillows in your bag."

She handed him her mug and he piled up everything from the mess kits. Balancing it all, he went to the opening of the cave and the flow of air through that gap chilled the bare skin of his legs. Lucky for them, however, since that ventilation kept the cave free of the smoke and other toxins from their fire.

Easing through the gap, he used the rainwater to rinse off their plates and after, to clean the coffee pot and refill it for the morning.

His shirt was damp by the time he was done and he shivered. At his pack, he pulled off his shirt and grabbed a dry sweatshirt, slipping it on.

Macy had also changed into a different sweatshirt and lay by the fire, watching him. Her gaze was wickedly tempting as he imagined lying beside her and shedding the clothes they were both using as defenses against their emotions.

He padded back to the fire and gave it one last poke. He would have to keep an eye on it during the night to make sure it was under control. Then he slipped into the sleeping bag beside her and lay his head on one of the pillows she had inflated.

A nice comfort considering the hard ground beneath them and the tarp which crinkled noisily as they moved about. Of course, he'd slept in worse conditions.

"It's not so bad. We're warm and dry," he said, striving for neutral.

"I'm still a little chilled," she admitted.

"We could zip the bags together and share our body heat," he said before his brain had a second to think about the consequences of those actions.

Her eyebrows shot up in surprise at the suggestion and

worry settled onto her face. She bit at her bottom lip and mulled over the suggestion before finally saying, "Do you think that's a good idea?"

He thought about lying beside her. Remembered the press of her body against his last night and the softness of her cheek beneath his hand. He imagined the softness of her in other spots and immediately answered.

"It's probably the worst idea I've ever had."

She chuckled, shook her head and toyed with one of the ties on the sleeping bag. "I always knew you were an honest man."

Honest? An honest man might confess to what he was feeling and the conflicting emotions she roused in him. But then again, he was an honorable man and surprisingly, honor sometimes meant being less than honest.

"I guess I should be glad you feel that way about me."

Macy sensed hurt in his words and hadn't meant to cause it. Cupping his cheek, the rough beard on his face rasped the palm of her hand. "I didn't mean anything bad by it. I always admired you."

"Did you? Lots of women thought I wasn't a happily-ever-after kind of guy," he said.

She thought back to those days and the women he had dated—none of them had been the kind to have lasting relationships with. Except her. Which made her wonder aloud, "Why me?"

A flush stained his face and he looked away at her perusal. "Why you? That night, you mean? Why you and not someone else?"

The words escaped her on a tortured breath. "Yes, why me?"

He met her gaze then, his resolute and hard. "I dated the kind of girls who didn't want commitment, but I knew you were different. I knew you and Tim… I had wondered for a while what it would be like if it was you and me."

Much as she had questioned afterward what being with Fisher would have been like.

"Do you ever think about it now? I mean, with the teaching offer and all?"

She couldn't bear to look at him as she finished and concentrated on the ties of the sleeping bag, twirling them around and around her finger as she waited for his answer.

And then waited some more.

Finally, she had no choice but to meet his gaze.

"What do you think?" he asked.

"I'd like to think that maybe you had thought about it. About us," she finally admitted, deciding that after eighteen years of doubt, it was time to put an end to it.

"I have, only now there's T.J. to consider as well. A son that I didn't know I had."

"I'm sorry that I didn't tell you before. With Tim's death and all that started happening afterward, I wasn't sure T.J. could handle that kind of revelation," she admitted.

"And now?" Fisher asked and tipped her face up so he could search her features. "What makes now any different?"

Tears filled her eyes. "I always worried whenever you went on a mission. I prayed for you to be safe so that maybe one day you and T.J. could get to know one another."

"Did you maybe pray a little for yourself? That maybe one day you and I—"

"Yes, I did," she blurted out and shifted closer to him. Cupped his cheek and brought her lips close. "I prayed that one day you and I could finish what we started."

"Then let's finish it," he replied and kissed her, taking

her lips over and over again until she was clinging to his shoulders. Pressing her body tight to his except the thickness and tangle of the sleeping bags kept them from really being close.

Without breaking the kiss, he unzipped both bags and dragged her body to his, his hands splayed against her back. The bare skin of their legs warm as they twined their legs together.

He needed to feel more of her skin and inched his hands beneath her sweatshirt. The flesh at the small of her back was damp. Slick as he moved his hands upward.

She copied his actions, shifting her hands beneath his shirt to grasp his back. Moaning impatiently before reaching back down for the hem of his shirt, in one swift move she had pulled it over his head, baring him to her gaze.

She stilled then as she laid her hands on his chest. They trembled for a moment before she eased her one hand down to the scar along his ribs—a stray piece of shrapnel and a minor injury. She ran her finger along that scar before shifting to another on his arm.

"Don't think about them. I'm here and I'm alive. I want to explore the feelings between us," he urged, knowing that if she focused on those old wounds for too long, her fear would overwhelm everything else.

"How about I think about the way your heart skips when I do this," Macy said and moved her hand to cup his pectoral muscle. Beneath her palm, his nipple hardened into a tight nub. She shifted her hand so she could strum her thumb across the hard peak.

He sucked in a breath and at her back, his hands clenched against her skin.

"Not fair, Mace."

"All's fair in love and war, Fisher. You should know that," she teased, bent her head and took his nipple into her mouth.

He cupped the back of her head to him and murmured his approval, but even as he did so, he slipped his hand between their bodies and cupped her naked breast. Rotated her nipple between his thumb and forefinger and she gasped against his chest.

"That feels good," she said.

"Then this will feel even better," he said and pulled her shirt up and over her head, encircled her waist and brought her breasts to his mouth, where he greedily suckled, shifting his lips from one breast to the other as he pleasured her.

She held his head to her, kissing his forehead and encouraging him with her soft sighs and the press of her hips against his hard body.

"Touch me, Mace," he pleaded.

She reached down between their bodies with her one hand and covered his erection. The cotton of his briefs was smooth over the long hard length of him. She ran her hand over him, but when he bumped his hips forward, she answered his silent plea.

She slipped her hand beneath the cotton and surrounded him with her hand. Stroked the smooth soft skin of his erection as he teethed the tip of her breast, yanking a harsh moan from her.

The sound of her passion and the gentle caress of her hand nearly undid him.

Fisher eased her onto her back and while he continued suckling her breasts, he moved his hand downward until he encountered the edge of her low-rise panties. She sucked in a breath and held it, creating a gap between her skin and the panties and he pressed forward, delving beneath the fabric. Moving beyond the soft curls between her legs to the center of her, where he stroked her with his fingers. Felt her swell and grow damp beneath his fingers until he shifted his hand downward and eased his finger within.

She arched her back and called out his name in a satisfied surprise. "Fisher. Please tell me this is about more than want."

"It's about more," he said.

Smiling, she brought her lips to his and said, "Then make love to me."

Chapter 20

He groaned, so loudly that it made his body rumble against hers. He jerked beneath her hand, clearly at the edge and threw his head back with a shuddering breath.

"Damn, Mace. I don't have any protection."

Tenderly she stroked him while with her other hand she cradled his jaw and urged him to face her once again. "I've been on the Pill since Tim got sick and just never stopped taking it, hopeful I would find love again. I'm safe."

"I'm safe also," he confirmed and there came a flurry of movement as they dragged off their underwear.

Spreading her legs, she guided him to her center where he poised for a moment, the tip of him brushing her nether parts. Her muscles clenched in anticipation of welcoming him. Accepting him into her warm depths.

He looked down to where they were about to join, leaving

her staring at the short dark strands of his hair. She needed more. She needed to see the look in his eyes as they took that step. As they started to finish what had begun eighteen years earlier.

Asserting gentle pressure on his jaw, she urged him to meet her emotionally the way he would soon join her physically.

His green eyes glittered brightly and a slight flush worked across his cheeks as he breached her center with just the tip of him, holding himself away from her with shaky arms.

"Are you sure?" he asked, almost as if he needed to convince himself as well.

"I've never been more sure of anything in my life," she said and flexed her hips downward, surrounding him as she did so.

They both held their breath at that union. Held steady as their bodies reunited and their minds processed the fact of that joining.

He was thick within her and hard. All of him was hard against her, she thought as she laid her hands on his shoulders. Stroked the broad width of them, broader even than he had been at twenty. Stronger.

"You feel..." She stopped, unable to find the words. How familiar and yet different in a way that was exciting, she thought as she ran her hands all across his well-defined arms and shoulders. Across the deep muscle in his chest and down the six-pack abs that came from real honest work and not a gym.

He held himself steady, allowing her that exploration before he braced his weight on one hand and picked up the other to caress her breast. He ran his thumb across the tip of her and then took her nipple between her thumb and forefinger, tenderly tweaked it, creating a pull deep within her legs that caressed him. Urged him to move.

Slowly he did, easing out with almost agonizing tardiness

before he stroked deep within again, pleasing her with the fullness of him and the friction of his movement.

Fisher gritted his teeth and held on for control. Nothing had prepared him for how good it would feel to be inside her. To have the warm wet depths of her hold him as he moved in and out of her body. As he stroked her breast and knew that just touching wasn't enough. He had to taste…all of her.

He bent his head and sucked her nipple into his mouth as he continued his tarried penetrations, drawing her ever closer to a release. She clutched his head to her, shifted her other hand down to his buttocks to urge him on, but he withdrew from her, wanting that taste.

At her protest, he trailed his mouth down the center of her. Over the softness of her flat midsection and the sweet indentation of her navel. He paused there to tongue that valley before quickly moving past the nest of darker brown curls between her legs and to the center of her.

She yanked in a ragged breath as he tongued the nub between her legs and eased his fingers into her. Stroking her as he then kissed her there and sucked, building her desire with his hands and mouth. Feeling the pulse of her passion intensify beneath his mouth and fingers until her back arched up off the ground and she came, calling his name and holding tight to his shoulders.

He feasted on that release with his mouth, but before it had ebbed, he quickly shifted upward and joined with her again.

"Fisher," Macy cried out, holding onto him as his penetration brought her to the edge again and she shuddered.

He smiled, bent his head and kissed her. She could taste herself on him and realized that now she wanted a taste as well.

Pushing on his shoulders, she urged him onto his back and

straddled him, increasing his penetration and her pleasure. It was all she could do not to come again, but then he cupped her breasts. Tweaked her taut nipples and urged her on.

"Come for me, Mace. Tell me how much you like this."

She shuddered and climaxed, the explosion of damp and sensation ripping deep between her legs.

"That's it, Mace," he said, but then groaned as she rocked her hips up and down on him, dragging all that moist pulsing heat along the hardness of his erection.

He brought his hands to her hips to guide her, helping her set a rhythm. Picking up his head to lick at her breasts as she rode him and built toward another climax, but she still wanted that taste before it happened.

She eased off him, earning a strangled protest until he realized her intent and then he lay back, offered himself up, laying his hands to his sides. Exposing every bit of him to her.

She started at his chest, licking and biting his deliciously brown male nipples while she encircled him and stroked him, the wet of her from her possession of him slick beneath her hand. As the trembling in his body increased with her caresses, she trailed her mouth down the center of him, but she paused to kiss the scar along his ribs and murmured.

"I never want you to be hurt again," she said, but even as she did so, she worried that she might be the one to cause that hurt if things didn't work out with them again.

Shifting downward, she traced the edges of his defined abdomen with her tongue before playfully biting the skin over his nearly flat navel. He chuckled and cupped the back of her head, urged her downward until her mouth brushed the tip of him.

His big body jumped beneath her and she slowed the stroke

of her hand, tightened her grasp as she finally took the head of him into her mouth.

He groaned then and closed his eyes, arched his back to ask for more and she gave it to him, sucking him deep into her mouth while continuing to fondle him with her hand until he inhaled roughly and held his breath. She tasted the first hint of his release, but knew she wanted him deep within her when he came. Wanted to come with him and share in their passion for one another.

She held him tight and straddled him again. Guided him to the center of her and then sank down on him.

Their gazes locked at that union and she leaned forward, grasped his hands where they rested at his sides and brought them up and over his head. Twining her fingers with his, she watched his face as she began to move. Welcomed the surprise and acceptance in his gaze as their bodies strove toward the same goal. As the rush of pleasure and satisfaction drew them closer and closer to release.

Her body was shaking as was his when she finally bent her head and brought her lips close to his. With her eyes locked on his intense gaze, she whispered, "Love me, Fisher."

"God help me, but I do, Mace. I love you," he said and released the explosion of passion between them.

The muted call of an early morning bird filtered into her brain followed by the hard warmth of him spooned against her. The cadence of his breath changed, confirming that he, too, was awakening. His body definitely was, she thought as his erection stirred against her buttocks, arousing fresh desire within her.

She hadn't thought it possible given how often they had made love throughout the night, but she couldn't deny it now.

Pressing herself against him, she waited expectantly.

"Are you sure?" he asked as he splayed his hand against her belly.

When she nodded and urged his hand downward, he eased his thigh between hers and then pressed his erection into her.

She was slightly dry and the friction of him was rough at first, but he stilled to allow her time to adjust. Found the center of her with his fingers, caressing her. Bringing his other hand around to tease her nipples until she was wet and throbbing around him.

He let her set the pace, murmuring encouragement as she rocked her hips back and forth, her movements slow at first, but growing more determined as he brought her to the edge with his hands.

As her strength flagged, he somehow rolled and brought them to their knees. She braced her arms on the ground and accepted the strong thrusts of his body which pushed her ever closer to her release.

When he leaned over her and cupped her breasts from behind, rotating her tight nipples with his fingers, she came roughly as did he. But he was still there to hold her. Support her as her body shook with the force of her climax until they both dropped to the ground, bodies still joined.

The passion ebbed from their bodies, but the comfort of being beside him remained. Bittersweet because she knew there were still many tests their reborn love would have to survive.

From outside came more morning sounds as the hill country awakened, but mixed in with those sounds was the distinctive patter of rain against the ground and rock face. Inhaling, she smelled the rain in the air and hoped that T.J.'d had the sense to remain in whatever shelter he had found.

She and Fisher would not have the same luxury.

They had to find T.J. and Sara and return to Esperanza in order to set things right. She hoped that by now Jericho had returned from his honeymoon. Before she could say anything, Fisher said, "I can feel you drifting away."

Almost prophetically, his body slipped from hers, breaking the physical connection of their bodies. Trying to deflect his concern, she said, "Only until we have time alone again."

"Will we have that kind of time again?" he pressed, not falling for her attempt to avoid any serious discussion.

She flipped onto her back and he pillowed his head on one hand, braced his elbow on the floor so he could face her. "I want to. Once we find the kids and deal with whatever is going on with them—"

"We'll deal with us? With telling T.J. the truth?"

She thought about how difficult that might be, but recognized it was well beyond time to confront that past history and heal those old wounds so they might build a future. If he wanted to build a future, that was.

"Will you think about the teaching position?"

He nodded. "I already had, but now it seems as if I have even more reason to consider it."

She wanted to press for more, but decided she already had received more of a promise than she had ever expected. Rising up, she dropped a kiss on his lips and afterward said, "We should get going."

As she went to move away, he eased his hand around the nape of her neck and dragged her close for a deeper kiss. She clung to him for a second before he finally broke away.

"Just to make sure you know" was all he said as he rose

and went to the fire, tossing on some kindling and firewood to ignite it once more.

Once a small flame sprung up, he kindled it while she dressed and stowed away their sleeping bags and pillows. By the time she turned back to him, he had also dressed, gotten the pot of coffee going and had some oatmeal with fruit cooking on the campfire grate.

"Smells good," she said and sat down on the tarp beside the mess kits he had cleaned the night before.

"It'll provide solid energy and chase away the chill from the rain."

It wasn't much longer before they were eating the delicious warm oatmeal and drinking the coffee. He had made enough in the pot to fill up a small thermos he had in his pack. With the ever present rain, it would feel nice to have something warm to drink once they were back on the trail.

She helped him clean up and finish putting away their supplies. Once again they slipped on the ponchos, careful that the plastic covered their packs. Using the hoods and their hats to shield their heads from the worst of the rain.

Outside the downpours from the night before had abated somewhat, but the ground beneath their feet was sloppy. It was immediately clear their climb today would be arduous.

Despite that, they pressed on, Fisher in the lead, constantly alert to the ground and area around them in the hopes of finding any sign of the teens. About two-thirds of the way up, almost within sight of the overlook, Fisher held up his hand and motioned for her to stop.

A few feet ahead of him was another gap in the rock face along the left of the trail. A big enough gap that he was able to enter with his pack on his back. She followed.

As in the earlier cave, a firepit rested in the middle of the space and beside the firepit, something heartbreakingly familiar.

She rushed to the stones near the pit and picked up the piece of bright silver foil. "It's T.J.'s favorite granola bar," she said.

Fisher knelt and motioned to the footprints all around the foot of the cave. "T.J.'s tread and Sara's smaller shoes from the looks of it."

He held his hand over the ashes and remnants of burnt wood surrounded by the stones of the makeshift firepit. "Still warm. They can't have left all that long ago. Maybe they were waiting during the morning for the rain to let up—"

"And when it didn't, they left. So maybe they're not so far ahead."

"Maybe," he said and jerked his head in the direction of the gap in the rock face. "Do you think you can pick up the pace?"

Her legs ached from the constant sucking and pulling of the mud as they hiked, but if it meant finding T.J. faster…

"I'll go whatever speed you want."

With a nod, he rose and walked toward the break, but he stopped before her, cradled her cheek and said, "I always said you were a hell of a woman."

She smiled at the compliment, gratified by his praise. Back out on the trail, however, she was sorely tempted to curse him as he took her up on her word and pushed her at a grueling pace. Finally the trail leveled off a bit. Luckily, the sun was trying to poke through the clouds. While it would bring heat and humidity, it would hopefully dry up the ground for an easier hike.

They were near a bend that would put them on the final part of the trail to the overlook when she heard what sounded like a shout and the sudden intense roar of rushing water. Fisher must have heard it as well since he hurried around the bend.

She followed and smacked into him since he had stopped dead on the trail. As she glanced ahead, she realized the reason why.

Barely twenty feet before them was a wide arroyo spanned by a rickety wooden footbridge.

On the footbridge were two people—T.J. and Sara—hanging onto the flimsy wood and rope balusters of the bridge as it swayed and bucked from the force of the water cascading across it and down the arroyo.

"T.J.!" she shouted and rushed toward the bridge.

Chapter 21

Fisher took off after Macy, fearful that she would attempt to cross the bridge to reach the teens.

He had barely gone a few feet when a sickening crack and groan filled the air as the moorings for the footbridge closest to them gave way.

The end of the bridge rushed downward, propelled by the flood waters while T.J. and Sara bravely clung to the ropes and what remained of the bridge. The remnants of the bridge, with them hanging onto it, slammed into the far side of the arroyo, nearly unsettling the teens. The rush of the water covered them and the bridge pieces and then with another loud snap, the other end of the bridge likewise collapsed, plunging the teens into the flood waters.

Since the water sluicing down the arroyo actually brought them closer to where he stood, he jumped off the trail and careened almost wildly down the slope toward the edges of the arroyo. Seconds later, as he reached the bank and searched for T.J. and Sara, he heard Macy pound down the slope behind him.

"Do you see them?" she shouted over the loud noise of the raging flash flood that continued to surge down the arroyo.

On the opposite bank was a tangle of wood and rope from the footbridge, caught up in some tree roots and rocks. He thought he saw a glimmer of a red jacket amongst the debris, but couldn't be sure.

Tossing off his poncho and pack in the event he would have to go in after the teens, he waded into the edge of the waters. The immense force of the current pulled at him. Cursing under his breath because he doubted he could make it across the flood waters to the remnants of the footbridge, he withdrew back to drier land.

As he did so, some of the remaining bits of bridge gave way and were swept down the arroyo, but luckily, it revealed that T.J. and Sara were directly opposite them, clinging to each other.

When he looked at them more closely, he realized that T.J. had managed to grab hold of a sapling that had been along the edge of the arroyo. T.J. had one arm around the sapling and another beneath Sara's arms. The young girl was clutching him frantically, holding on to his arm and the fabric of T.J.'s red windbreaker.

He had to act and quickly. Sara looked like she couldn't hold on for much longer and the torrent of the waters was quickly eroding the ground securing the sapling.

He untied his rope from his pack and formed a lasso. He was a bit rusty, he thought, as he twirled the rope round and round, building up enough force to then toss it out across the twenty or so feet separating them from the teens.

It fell short of the mark but was in the right general vicinity.

He quickly reeled the rope back in, once again twirled the lasso over and over until he let it sail and it landed smack between the teens.

T.J. shouted at Sara to grab the rope and she did, but Fisher had other ideas.

"Tie it around the two of you—"

"The water's too strong and we'll be too heavy," T.J. shouted back. "Take Sara across first."

"T.J., please," Macy shouted from beside him, but he glanced at her and said, "T.J.'s right. It'll be too hard and we'll lose them both."

Macy hated that the two men were right. She also hated that by pulling Sara across first, they might risk T.J.'s life if he lost his shaky grasp on the small tree. But continuing to argue only increased the risk of that happening.

"Hold on tight, Sara," she shouted out and watched as one-handedly, her son somehow managed to get the rope up and around Sara's arms, securing her to the lasso.

Fisher had tied the other end of the rope around a tree on the bank and as T.J. released Sara, the waters carried her downward. Fisher began to pull her in, the muscles in his arms straining as he battled the force of the waters.

He had her halfway across the arroyo when a shot rang out.

By his head, a bit of bark flew off the tree beside him.

Someone was shooting at them, she realized, but she hadn't even finished the thought when Fisher blocked her body with his and continued reeling in Sara.

Another shot rang out, close to his head once again. He mumbled a curse, pushed her back behind the protection of the tree trunk while he held on to the rope, fighting to not lose his grip on it.

"Can you handle the rope?" he said and she immediately grabbed it, sensed the pull of the water and Sara's weight threatening to drag it from her hands.

She dug in forcefully, firmly planting her feet in the wet soil and leaning back to get the leverage she needed while Fisher grabbed his rifle. As she pulled in the rope, dragging it in hand over hand, Fisher used the scope to search for the shooter.

Another shot rang out, dangerously close to Fisher, but he grunted with apparent satisfaction.

"Now, I've got the bastard," he said and opened fire.

Her arms trembled from the force she was exerting, but she kept at it, protected by Fisher's body and shooting.

As Sara neared the bank of the arroyo, the muddy dirt by her feet flew up.

The shooter had turned his attention to her.

Fisher reacted immediately, rushing to block Sara's body with his and urge her in the direction of the tree.

Sara plopped down behind the trunk, shivering from the cold of the water. Her hands shook as she slipped the rope from around her body and handed it to Macy.

Wet hair covered most of her face, but her fear was evident. Her teeth chattered from the cold as she said, "Y-y-ou n-n-eed t-t-o get T-t-J."

She peered across the surging waters cascading down the arroyo. T.J. was still holding onto the sapling, but he was deeper in the water as the roots of the tree began to give way.

She didn't have much time to save her son.

To save their son.

While Fisher continued to pin down the shooter by returning fire, she undid the rope from around the tree and stepped toward the bank of the arroyo. Fisher shifted his body to keep her covered. She swung the rope as hard as she could and when she thought she had enough momentum, released it.

It flew across the waters but landed below T.J.'s position.

Mumbling a curse, she quickly pulled the rope back in and gave it another try, aiming for a spot well above him.

As the rope flew across the waters this time, it landed a half a dozen or so feet above and was quickly carried downward by the waters.

With a sickening knot in her stomach, she watched T.J. lunge outward with one hand for the rope. As he did so, the sapling in his other hand gave way and he surged down the arroyo. She feared she had lost him, but suddenly there came the rough pull of the rope in her hands. Strong enough to almost upend her, but she braced herself and wrapped the rope around her arm.

T.J. had managed to grab the rope.

Using all her might, she made her way back to the tree and braced herself against the tree. She used the trunk to help her, inching around the tree with the rope. Suddenly Sara was beside her, helping her to tie the rope to the tree.

Then another shot hit the trunk beside them, gouging a deep wound in the wood, but Fisher was immediately shooting at their assailant, trying to protect them.

As Fisher returned fired, she and the young teen began to reel in T.J. Together they managed to bring him onto the bank and once he was there, he slogged out of the water and mud and rushed to their side.

The happy reunion was short-lived, however, as the shooter opened fire on them again.

The three of them ducked down behind the meager protection of the tree and Fisher.

Fisher kept firing on the location of the shooter. It was only a matter of time before someone got hurt since they were too exposed on the banks of the arroyo. If he could backtrack on the trail and get behind the shooter, he could disarm them.

Glancing back at Macy where she huddled with the two kids, he said, "Can you grab the rifle and cover me? I need to take out that shooter."

Macy vehemently shook her head. "I'm a suck shot."

"I'll do it. My dad taught me how to shoot," T.J. said, standing up and holding out his hand for the rifle.

He ignored the ache in his gut at T.J.'s mention of his dad. Of Tim. Of how it could have been him who had taught T.J. to shoot the same way his dad had taught him and Jericho.

Driving away the pain, he handed T.J. the rifle and then stood beside him to point out the location of the shooter. Luckily, their attacker decided to fire, providing a needed view of his muzzle fire to confirm his position. T.J. immediately returned fire, his shot striking on the rock right by where he had seen the muzzle fire.

"Great shot. Keep that up, son," he said and patted the teen on the back. "I'm going to double-back along the trail and then come up behind the shooter."

"I'll cover you."

He nodded. "As soon as I've got a hold of him, I'll signal you so you can come down."

T.J. confirmed that he understood and then Fisher shot a look at Macy as she huddled next to Sara behind the tree trunk, trying to comfort the young girl. As their gazes met, he gave her a look that hopefully communicated his intent to stay safe.

At her nod, he rushed back up the slope and to the trail. While he did so, he whipped his cell phone out and called down to the ranger station, advising them of what was happening. Although the ranger immediately answered, he gave Fisher the answer he suspected.

"The sheriff and I won't be able to reach you any time soon," the ranger advised.

"I understand. He's got three of us pinned down and I need to get this shooter under control."

"Understood. The sheriff and I will be on our way shortly."

"I'll keep you posted," Fisher said and tucked the phone back into his pocket.

During the conversation, he had managed to make it halfway down to where the shooter was located. Moving as quickly as he could along the sloppy trail, he kept his eyes focused on the shooter. Listened as the ping and ricochet of gunfire echoed through the hills and arroyo.

Well aware of the shooter's position, he slipped from the trail, careful to stay out of view of their attacker, but unfortunately, he knew he might be out of view of T.J. and Macy. It meant he would likely need to deal with the shooter on his own, but he was well-prepared to do that.

In retrospect, it was the only way to keep them safe which was all important to him.

Important enough to risk his life.

With that awareness, he forged ahead.

Chapter 22

T.J. had his one arm propped against the trunk of the tree which shielded the bulk of his body from the shooter. The rifle was up against his other arm and he kept up a steady, but careful return of fire. Macy nestled with Sara behind the tree.

The girl was shivering in her arms and softly whispering, "It's all my fault."

Macy did what she could to comfort and reassure her. "It's no one's fault, Sara. Don't worry. We'll be fine."

She suddenly heard the hollow click as T.J. fired. The rifle was empty. Ducking down next to them in the meager protection provided by the tree trunk, he quickly reloaded the weapon with the ammo she had removed from Fisher's pack. Then he rapidly reassumed his position and began a brisk return of fire.

When he paused for a moment, she glanced up at him and asked, "Is something wrong?"

"I'm not sure. I think I saw Mr. Yates for a moment." He kept his weapon trained on the attacker, but held his fire.

She only hoped the shooter had not seen Fisher as well. When there was a continued lull in the shots from down below, T.J. dropped back down next to her and said, "We should head down. See if Mr. Yates needs our help."

"I'll go for the trail first. If it's clear, then you and Sara can follow," she instructed.

As she was about to move back up to the footpath, T.J. resumed his position at the tree, ready to fire, but no one shot at her as she headed up the embankment and back to the trail.

The ground was slippery and the weight of her pack made speed of any kind laborious, but she couldn't delay.

Fisher might need help.

Ironic how in all the years that she had worried about him being killed while on a tour of duty, he was probably in greater danger right here at home because of her and T.J.

She forced such negative thoughts from her mind and focused on the trail, remembering where she had last seen Fisher before he left the footpath to double back on the shooter. From behind her came the sounds of T.J. and Sara plodding along, gaining ground on her.

The lack of shooting was almost as scary as being fired upon. *Had Fisher subdued their assailant?* she wondered, refusing to consider the other possibility as she paused at the edge of the trail. She peered back up at where they had been pinned down by the shooter. It seemed far enough down and as she took the first step off the trail, she noticed that a few feet away, the brush and soil was torn up, as if someone had recently come that way.

Fisher, she thought, and rushed downward, at one point

losing her footing and ending up on her backside, sliding down the muddy bank of the trail. The weight of the pack dragged at her as she struggled to rise and she opted to release the bindings keeping it on.

She could move more quickly without it and if Fisher needed her help ...

Free of the encumbering weight, she charged forward and came upon a small clearing where Fisher was fighting with a bigger, but slightly older man. A man who still held a rifle and was trying to bring it around to shoot.

"Fisher!" she called out and raced ahead.

Macy shouted his name and from the corner of his eye, he saw her plowing toward them, heedless of the fact that their attacker still had his weapon. Putting herself in danger.

The larger man took advantage of that millisecond of distraction and sharply hammered the butt of the rifle into his ribs. The blow drove the air from him, but he couldn't let the pain or lack of breath hold him back.

He had been tempering his actions up until now, keeping from using deadly force in the hopes of subduing the man, but Macy's presence had changed all that.

His years of military training took over.

When the man swung around to try and raise the rifle to fire, he unleashed a roundhouse kick to the man's head which dazed him for a moment. He followed up with a penetrating jab to the man's solar plexus, but the man somehow kept his hold on the rifle.

Charging him head on, he tackled their assailant to the ground and the impact of the landing finally loosened the man's hold on the weapon which went sailing a few feet away.

"Mom," he heard as he wrestled the man to his stomach and got him in a choke hold. Applying pressure, the cartilage in the man's neck crunched beneath his arm. With just a little more pressure it would give and end the battle. But as he shot a look out of the corner of his eye, he realized that T.J. and Sara had arrived. T.J. had shouldered the rifle again and now had it trained on them, ready to fire.

"It's okay, son. I've got him under control," he said and loosened his grip on the man's throat while grabbing hold of the arm he had twisted behind the man's back.

"Get his rifle, Mace," he instructed and she did so, picking up the discarded weapon before resuming a spot a few feet away beside the teens.

"Get up," he commanded the man, although he dragged him upward as well and maintaining his grip, made him face Macy and the teens.

"Dad!" Sara exclaimed, stepping from behind T.J. to stare at the man he had subdued.

He finally allowed himself the luxury of examining the man and realized he was one and the same as the picture that he and Macy had found online of Howard Engeleit.

Macy realized it as well. She stepped forward and looked up at him. Shook her head and said, "You're Sara's dad. You were shooting at your own daughter? Why?"

Engeleit sneered at Sara and said, "Because that little bitch is just like her mother. She was going to ruin my life."

Fisher increased his pressure on the man's arm, forcing him up onto his tiptoes to avoid the pain. As he did so, he asked, "Care to explain in a little more detail?"

"Sara saw my wife and I arguing—"

"You were always screaming at us and then you hit her. I

had to do something and realized I had my cell phone camera. I recorded him yelling and hurting my mom."

Howard sagged in his arms and his tone was pleading as he said, "You didn't understand what was going on, Sara. It was all a misunderstanding."

"I know what I saw," she shot back. "You were abusing mom and you were lying to the judge about her being unfit," she immediately continued and advanced on him until she stood right before him. She was petite and Howard's big bulk nearly dwarfed her, but she got up on her tiptoes until she was right in his face and said, "You only wanted custody of me so you could keep her quiet about how you mistreated us. But now I have proof of what you are."

Even though Fisher had a firm hold on him, the man lunged at his daughter. He yanked him back and T.J. took a protective step forward, the rifle pointed right at the man's head.

Howard stepped away and as if finally realizing that he was defeated, drooped in Fisher's arms until he was on his knees, his head downcast as he bemoaned his likely fate. "You're going to spoil everything, Sara. Once people see that video, I'll be ruined."

It was T.J. who spoke up next. "The night of the accident, someone chased us. Sara thought it was you."

Howard shook his head. "It was one of my investigators. I had him trying to find Sara. I just wanted you home safe and sound, honey," he cried, his tone cajoling, but Sara remained unconvinced.

"What you wanted was my cell phone with the video, that's why you tried to take it from me. You said you'd kill me if I didn't give it to you."

She faced Macy. "That's why I ran away and why I had those bruises on my arms—from fighting him off." She reached into her pocket and pulled out the cell phone. She had put it into a plastic bag and despite her soaking from the rain and flood waters, the cell phone appeared undamaged.

She dangled the bag with the phone in front of her dad. "Even if you take it now, it won't do you any good. T.J. and Joe helped me upload a copy of the video. It's safe now and I'm going to give it to Mom. I hope the judge gives her everything she's asking for in the divorce."

"And we're going to show it to the police," Macy said, coming to stand beside the young girl. She placed her arm around Sara's shoulders and said, "It's going to be all right now."

The young teen nodded. "It is. Thanks to T.J. and all of you, I finally feel safe."

From across the distance separating them, Macy met Fisher's gaze and the pride on it was evident. Their son had only been trying to keep Sara protected all that time. She only wished he had trusted them so they could have avoided a lot of misunderstandings and the risk to their lives.

"We should get down to the ranger station," she said and Fisher inclined his head in T.J.'s direction. T.J. had shouldered his pack for the trip down the trail.

"There's cable ties in the top pouch to the left, Macy. If you can get some, I'll get ol' Howard here trussed up for the trip down the hillside."

While T.J. continued to keep his rifle trained on Howard, she quickly removed the cable ties and handed them to Fisher who expertly secured Howard's hands behind his back.

After he was done, he said, "I'll take the pack now, T.J."

"I can handle it. Why not take Mom's?" he said and with a nod, Fisher shouldered the smaller pack as well as Engeleit's rifle which he used to prod the man and get him moving down the trail. As he walked, he called ahead to the ranger station to apprise the ranger of what had happened. When he hung up, he said to them, "The sheriff will be waiting for us down at the bottom of the trail."

She nodded and took up a spot just behind him while T.J. brought up the rear, Fisher's rifle cradled in his arms.

The downhill journey took a few hours, but it was much shorter and easier than the uphill climb. The sun had finally emerged, bringing with it the heat and humidity which she had expected, but also drying the ground somewhat, making their footing and journey less severe.

At the end of the trail, the local sheriff and park ranger were waiting for them. The sheriff took Howard Engeleit into custody, promising them that he would make sure Engeleit was held without bail in light of the threat he posed to Sara and his attempt to murder them along the trail.

With the sheriff gone, the ranger offered them the use of the ranger station to rest a spell before they went home.

Macy wanted nothing more than to head to Esperanza and clear up things about T.J., hopefully with Jericho and not Deputy Rawlings. But before she did that, she realized something else needed to be done.

She faced Fisher and held out her hand. He took it with his and smiled gently, although a hint of confusion colored his features. "I want to thank you for everything you've done for us."

T.J. stepped up to his mother's side, placed his arm around her shoulders and said, "Yes, thank you for taking care of my mom and me, Mr. Yates. I know my dad would have appreciated all you did also."

A pained look crossed Fisher's features and Macy knew it was the right time to act. Turning to her side, she took hold of her son's hand and said, "There's something you need to know, T.J."

Before either she or Fisher could say anything else, T.J. surprised them by saying, "Mr. Yates is my biological father, isn't he?"

Once again pain flashed across Fisher's features, but he schooled his emotions quickly. With a nod, he said, "Yes, I am. How did you know?"

Sara jumped in at the moment to say, "I think you all need some time alone. I'll be waiting in the ranger station."

After she walked away, T.J. said, "While we were on the steps of the church, I overheard someone say how handsome father and son looked. They were talking about you and me. Then I realized how much we looked alike. How we were standing alike."

And as they stood there facing one another, Macy once again noted the physical similarities between the two that marked them as father and son. Guilt swamped her, creating a knot in her stomach. She took a deep breath and slowly released it before she said, "I'm sorry you learned the truth that way. Your dad... Tim and I should have told you."

"Tim Ward was my father," T.J. began, his voice shaking with emotion.

Fisher laid a hand on T.J.'s shoulder and the young man didn't pull away. A good sign, he thought.

"Tim Ward was a good man. I never want to replace him in your heart, T.J. But I would like to get to know you."

Beneath his hand, tension radiated in T.J.'s body, but then the teen relaxed a bit. After a moment's delay, T.J. nodded and said, "I'd like that."

He didn't know how it happened, but a second later, they

were embracing and his heart swelled with love and pride at the fact that this young man was his son. "I'm proud of how you protected Sara and helped me up on the trail."

"Thank you for all that you did for us. For helping Mom, Sara and me," T.J. replied again before easing away to stand before Macy.

She slipped her arm around his shoulders and gave him a hug. "You're welcome to visit any time you'd like, Fisher. I know that with your military life that may not—"

"Actually, I may be seriously considering that job up at West Point," he said, wanting her to know that things had changed between them. Aware that in time, he might be asking her and T.J. to go with him, although he kept that to himself for the moment. Too much was happening right now to add that to the mix.

"I'm glad, Fisher. I always worried about you when you went on tour," she said and added, "It's time we all headed home."

"Let's go get Sara and maybe get the two of you into some dry clothes," Fisher suggested.

"I lost my pack with all our stuff when the bridge gave out," T.J. said.

Fisher motioned to his bag and Macy's which were on the ground by T.J.'s feet. "The clothes may be big, but you and Sara can take stuff from our packs."

T.J. immediately grabbed one pack and went off in the direction of the ranger station, his long strides quickly putting some distance between them. Fisher picked up the other pack and together, and much more slowly, he and Macy strolled to the station.

As they walked, she glanced up at him, almost shyly. "You were serious about considering that teaching position?"

He thought about leaving the life he had known for so long. A life that had brought him order, discipline and stability. But as he met Macy's gaze, he thought about all that he had missed with her and all that they could still have. With a smile and a nod, he said, "I've never been more serious about anything in my life."

Her smile was the only answer he needed.

Chapter 23

"I don't know what's going to happen with my mom and dad, so I'd like to stay on the ranch for now," Sara said, her brown-eyed gaze skittering over each of them before finally settling on T.J. as he sat beside Joe on the couch.

Jewel Mayfair contemplated Sara's request a moment before responding. "I hope the three of you realize how much danger you put yourselves in by not trusting us with the information about what was happening."

Macy watched as if almost orchestrated, the heads of all three teens bobbed up and down in unison. Bodies slouched, they were clearly aware of how their behavior had jeopardized not only their lives, but hers and Fisher's.

Jewel continued. "I have no problem with you staying as long as you'd like, Sara, but we need to let your mom know what's happened, and also Sheriff Yates."

"I've already talked to Jericho," Fisher offered from his spot beside her. "I phoned him from the ranger station, plus the local sheriff faxed him a copy of his report a short while ago. He'd like to interview all of you tomorrow so that he can complete his part of the report on Howard Engeleit's activities."

T.J. perked up and said, "Does that mean I'm no longer in trouble with the law?"

"You're out of trouble with them, but not with me," Jewel advised. Facing the two boys, she said, "Starting tomorrow, I expect both of you to get back to work bright and early. Even though you did what you did for a good reason, T.J. still needs to pay off his mom for the damage to the two cars and the speeding ticket."

Jewel then faced Macy, "Don't you agree?"

"Wholeheartedly," she said with a nod.

"I'm glad that's settled. I'd like to talk to Macy and Fisher alone for a moment, but afterward we're going to call your mom, Sara."

The young girl nodded and the three teens rose and went off to the family room to join the other kids, while Fisher and she remained behind in the library.

Jewel rose and closed the door, let out a tired sigh. "Am I glad that's all over."

"So am I. I'm sorry about how T.J. acted," she began, but Jewel waved her off and sat back down in her chair.

"He was confused and trying to help. Luckily it worked out well, only…I had actually thought we'd find him and Sara somewhere on the ranch property."

Fisher shifted to the edge of the couch and leaned his elbows on his thighs. His large hands were clasped before him as he said, "Why do you say that?"

"For several nights I've been restless with worry about T.J. and Sara and have been going for walks outside. For the past few nights I've heard noises while I walked. What sounded like crying—"

"Like what you heard before that you mentioned to Clay Colton?" she asked.

Jewel confirmed it with a shake of her head. "Similar, only this time I thought I heard hushed voices as well which is why I thought it might be the teens."

"Did you call Jericho and tell him?" Fisher asked.

Jewel shrugged and said, "I figured he had enough on his plate what with his just getting back from his honeymoon and all that was happening with the kids. Besides, when I mentioned it to Clay again, he said he would check around once more."

Fisher shifted back onto the sofa beside her. "If it continues, you should mention it to Jericho. It could be nothing or it could be—"

"Serious. I know. I should listen to the advice I gave the kids and talk to the sheriff about it."

Macy considered what her friend and boss had said and grew concerned that the noises might truly be something to worry about. "Do you want Fisher and me to stay here tonight? Help you keep an eye on things?"

Jewel shook her head. "No need right now. Clay is going to look around, but if it keeps up, I'll call Jericho. Besides, I figure the two of you need some time together. Or am I wrong about that?"

Hesitant, she risked a glance in Fisher's direction, but there was no uncertainty there. He quickly answered, "You wouldn't be wrong about that, Jewel. There's a lot for me and Macy to work on."

A broad smile came to Jewel's face. "Well, I'm glad to hear that. If you need to, take another day or so, Macy. Ana and I can handle the kids."

She appreciated her boss's offer and thanked her as she rose from the sofa. Turning to Fisher, she said, "I think it's time we took T.J. home and let Jewel get some rest."

Fisher stood up and eased his hand into hers. "I'd like to go home with you, if that's okay."

Macy grinned. "It's better than okay. It's what's right."

Fisher was used to sitting down to dinner with his men or his father and brother. Maybe it was because they were generally taciturn men that he found the back and forth between Macy and her son—no, their son—to be so lively.

T.J. was busy filling her in on what Joe had to report about the goings on during his absence.

"He says Deputy Rawlings was totally pissed off when Sheriff Yates told him that he was assuming control over Sara's case."

Macy carefully and methodically cut into the steak on her plate, clearly thoughtful about T.J.'s comments. "I think the Deputy is interested in Jewel, so maybe he had hoped to spend some more time around her thanks to the case."

"I don't like him," T.J. said without hesitation and then stuffed a chunk of sirloin in his mouth.

"That's understandable," he offered. "He was kind of rough on you."

"Damn straight," T.J. replied with a determined nod while he chewed the steak.

"T.J.," Macy warned, but the teen quickly swallowed and renewed his protest.

"He wouldn't cut me any slack, even when I told him the accident wasn't my fault."

"Let's just say he had past history to consider. Sometimes it's tough to overcome that kind of past although what you did for Sara will count for a lot," she said.

T.J. glanced over in his direction as if waiting for his take on things and then Macy looked his way as well. Considering T.J.'s actions that day, there was only one thing he could say.

"You were a hero today. You helped keep us all safe, only... Next time you should trust your mom more. Tell her if you or a friend are in trouble."

"What about you? Can I tell you if I'm in trouble?" he challenged and at his words, Macy looked away, obviously uncomfortable and possibly nervous about the answer.

To quell her discomfort, he laid his hand over hers as it rested on the table and said, "You can count on me, T.J. I'll be there if you need me."

"Will you be here for my mom?" he pressed and Macy's hand tensed beneath his.

"Your mom and I...there's lots for us to discuss and whether I'm here, that's for your mom to decide."

T.J. shot a glance between the two of them, without a doubt wondering about them, but he kept silent and resumed eating.

He and Macy did the same, polishing off the rest of the quick and simple steak and potatoes meal they had prepared.

After dinner, T.J. helped clear off the table and then walked to the door of the kitchen. "I'm kind of tired, so I'm going to my room to turn in early."

Fisher thought about saying goodnight. Thought about leaving the two of them that evening and every evening thereafter. It was more difficult to imagine than he had expected.

Macy solved the problem for him, coming to stand by his side while addressing T.J. "Would you mind if Fisher stayed with us tonight?"

"With us?" T.J. echoed and then picked up a finger and pointed it between the two of them. "You mean, like with the two of you like a mom and dad kind of stay with us?"

Heat flared across his face and as he shot a glance out of the corner of his eye, he realized Macy was likewise blushing at T.J.'s directness. Despite that, she nodded and answered, "Yes. As in Fisher and me staying together tonight like a mom and dad."

T.J. thought about it for a moment before he said, "Could I speak to Mr. Yates for a second, man-to-man?"

With a nod, Fisher walked up to him and then the two of them stepped outside the kitchen and into the hall. T.J. stood face-to-face with him and he was struck once again by how much the boy looked like him and wondered why no one had ever noticed before or if they had, why they hadn't said anything.

"What can I do for you, T.J.?" he asked, his voice pitched low so that Macy would not hear.

"You do mean to do what's right for my mom, don't you?" the boy asked, his tones seriously adult.

"I do, but I also want to do what's right for you. I've been thinking about whether to accept a teaching position at West Point—"

"I think Mom would like that," T.J. said and then quickly added, "And so would I. It would let me get a fresh start somewhere and get ready for college. That is if I'm included in your plans."

He imagined what T.J. might feel like, being faced with so much change in so short a time. So much life altering change, but then he realized he didn't have to imagine so hard. He had lived through such upheaval when his mom had abandoned them. He was living through the same abrupt change now with the discovery that he had a son and was still in love with Macy.

Even with his own confusion about the recent changes, he had no doubt about the answer to T.J.'s question.

"You're my son and I want what's best for you. If you and your mom wanted to stay here until you finished high school—"

"I'll do whatever will make Mom happy. I know I haven't made her life easy lately, only…I really missed Dad…Mr. Ward…"

"Your dad. Tim Ward was your dad, T.J., but I'd like for us to get to know one another. For your mom and I to possibly share our lives as well."

T.J. nodded and before Fisher could anticipate it, the teen hugged him hard, but then just as swiftly, turned and raced up the stairs.

Emotion swelled up in him, so strong it nearly choked him. Taking a few steadying breaths, he walked into the kitchen where Macy had just about finished cleaning up. As she dried her hands on a dish towel, she faced him. Worry clouded her features as she asked, "Is everything okay?"

He smiled and said, "Better than I could have expected."

"Really?" She walked toward him, stopped about a foot away and looked up at him. "T.J. is…okay with things?"

"As long as you're okay with things, only you and I really haven't decided what the future holds for us."

Macy was nearly strangling the dish towel in her hands and he stepped up and took it from her. "Why don't we go up to your room and talk."

She narrowed her eyes, as if taking his measure. "Is talk all you want to do?"

He grinned. "What do you think?"

Taking the final step to close the distance between them, she slipped her index finger beneath the waistband of his jeans and tugged him even closer. "I think that if you don't plan on kissing me soon, I may go crazy."

Clay Colton glanced out over the Hopechest Ranch from the small hill at the edge of the Bar None. All seemed quiet down below and he had yet to hear the strange noises in the night about which Jewel had complained.

Pressing forward, he headed down the incline to the metal fence which separated the two ranches and helped keep his livestock from wandering off. He followed the fence line, thinking that possibly one of his animals or even a wild animal had gotten caught up in the fencing. Or maybe they had been hurt by the barbed wire and lay injured nearby, accounting for the crying sounds that Jewel had heard.

Riding slowly along the fence, he kept his eyes trained for signs of any animals or possible problems and then something caught his eye in the bright moonlight.

He eased off Crockett and ground tethered the horse as he approached the fence. Squatting down, he realized there were boot prints near the fence and also, a few cigarette butts close by. He picked up one of the butts. There was something familiar about it, although he couldn't quite put a handle on what it was.

Taking a bandanna from his back pocket, he slipped that butt and two others into the bandanna, intending to show them to Jericho. As he stood and tucked the bandanna into his pocket, something glinted in the moonlight once more up ahead on the fence.

As he approached, he realized that the bottom line of barbed wire had been cut. Recently, since the ends were still silvery and unrusted like the rest of the wire. With the bottom wire cut, it would be easy for an animal or a person to slip through and as he looked around more carefully, he noticed more boot prints on the Hopechest side of the fence.

Strange, he thought and rose, searched out the countryside for signs of any strays or humans, but saw no one. He did notice, however, that he was near some caves where he and his kid brother Ryder had used to play as children. They would head down into the caves to avoid the heat of the summer day and had even camped out overnight in one of the larger ones a time or two.

He and Ryder had sure shared some fun times back then, before the problems.

His baby brother Ryder, he thought once again as he had often thought about him in the past few weeks. He'd had no luck reaching him in the prison where he was being kept. No luck finding out anything about how his brother was doing.

As he let out a low whistle for Crockett and the horse came over, he thought about writing to Ryder once more, but then decided that it would probably be another futile endeavor. Grabbing Crockett's reins and hoisting himself back up in the saddle, he decided he had to do something more if he was going to find out what was up with his little brother.

Tomorrow he would phone the prison and after, head into town to tell Jericho about his findings along the fence. He

hoped his friend would be able to help him figure out what
was going on between the Bar None and the Hopechest and
possibly decide what to do about Ryder.

Chapter 24

Macy held Fisher close, arching her back as he slowly shifted in and out of her, slowly building her climax.

As she reached the edge and sucked in a rough breath, he stopped and arms braced on either side of her, looked down at her. "Are you okay?"

She was more than okay, but there was T.J. to consider just a few doors away. Reaching up, she cradled the back of his head and urged him down until she could murmur softly against his lips, "More than okay, love."

He kissed her then and whispered, "I understand, Mace."

He continued kissing her as he began to move within her again, dragging her to the edge time and time again, holding his own release back until his body was shaking above her. Raising her hips, she deepened his penetration and dragged a rough moan from him which she muffled with another kiss.

"Come with me," she urged against his mouth and with a few stronger strokes, he did, joining her as her release washed over her. Swallowing her small scream of satisfaction with another kiss before he lowered himself onto her, breathing heavily.

It took a minute or so before they could move, easing onto their sides so they were facing one another. It took less than that before they were touching each other again.

As Fisher cupped her breast and shifted his thumb back and forth across the tip of it, he said, "I can't get enough of you, Mace. I can't imagine how I survived all this time being without you."

"I'm here now, Fisher," she said and ran the back of her hand over the ridges of his abdomen before moving lower and encircling his softness which immediately began to harden beneath her hand.

He stilled his motions and as she glanced up at him, he asked, "I want more than now, Mace. Can you give that?"

"Whatever you decide, I'll be here for you, Fisher. I don't want to lose you again."

He groaned once more and his body shook against hers from the force of his emotion.

"You won't lose me, Mace. I promise," he said and pressed her down into the mattress as he began loving her anew.

Macy held him tight, her hands clasped on his shoulders. Her body welcoming his as they tried to make up for all the time they had lost. As she tried to store up the memories to keep her in the event he decided to go back on another tour of duty.

He must have felt her stiffen in his arms since he bent his head and repeated his earlier promise. "You won't lose me."

As she released her heart and body to him, she prayed that was a promise he could keep.

Jericho flipped through the pile of envelopes that Clay had handed him. Each bore Ryder's name and cell number neatly printed in Clay's handwriting. He noticed that the postmarks on the envelopes went back for several months. Leaning back in his chair, he rubbed his finger across his lips and contemplated the man sitting before him.

Clay Colton sat tensely on the edge of the hard wooden chair, juggling his Stetson between his large work-worn hands.

"You say the warden had nothing to tell you."

Clay nodded and released a heavy sigh. "Warden said he wouldn't tell me anything about Ryder and couldn't give me a reason why the letters had been returned unopened."

Even though Ryder's actions years earlier had created a rift between the two brothers, Jericho had no doubt that Clay sincerely wanted to make amends and was concerned about his younger brother. Unfortunately, there wasn't much he could offer for the moment.

"I'd take a ride to the prison and demand to speak to the warden and Ryder. Hear what they've got to say to your face. In the meantime, I'll make some calls and see what I can find out."

A tight smile came to Clay's lips. "I'd appreciate that." He juggled the hat up and down once more, clearly uneasy.

"Something else you want to say?" Jericho asked.

"I hate doing this to you so soon after your return, but I'm a little worried about something I found up at the border between the Bar None and the Hopechest."

The other man explained about Jewel's concerns about the

crying noises in the night and how he had gone out and discovered the boot prints, cigarette butts and the recently cut fence.

"Rustlers, you think?" Jericho asked, but Clay emphatically shook his head.

"All my horses are accounted for and I've asked around. No one's missing any livestock or seen anything out of the ordinary."

A relief, Jericho thought. With him and Olivia just back from their honeymoon and still recovering from their run-in with Allan Daniels, he had been looking forward to a little quiet at his return. Of course, given all that had been going on with T.J., Macy and Fisher, quiet was the last thing that it seemed he was going to get.

"I'll send the deputy to make some extra rounds at night and take a ride up myself to see what's happening. I'll let you know what I make of things."

Clay rose from his chair and held out his hand. "I'd appreciate whatever you could do on both counts."

He stood, shook Clay's hand and nodded. As Jericho was sitting back down, he noticed Fisher coming through the front door of the sheriff's office.

"Welcome, bro," he called out and waved his brother over to his door.

Fisher seemed tired and considering what had happened during the last few days, it was understandable. But as Fisher approached the door, he noticed the happy gleam in his brother's eyes. When they embraced, there was something more relaxed in his brother's normally militarily rigid posture.

"It's good to have you home, Jericho," Fisher said and after, sat in the chair before his desk.

"You seem to be doing okay, all things considered."

Fisher leaned his elbows on the arms of the chair and laced

his fingers together before him. "All things considered, I'm doing better than okay although..."

His brother surged forward in the chair, his hazel eyes glittering brightly. "There's a lot I've got to say and I'm going to ask you to let me finish it all before you start asking any questions."

Jericho nodded and leaned back in his chair which squeaked from the weight of his body. As he grasped the arms of the well-worn leather chair, the bright gold of his new wedding band caught Fisher's eye.

Once again he thought about how his brother hadn't seemed like the home and hearth type, but then again, until lately, he hadn't thought of himself that way.

That was, until lately.

"I'm thinking of taking the teaching position at West Point instead of signing up for another tour of duty in the Middle East. I'll miss my men and worry about them, but I think I can do a lot more good teaching new officers."

He waited for Jericho to comment, but his brother just sat there, although a broad smile slowly leaked onto his face.

"Nothing to say?"

"You told me not to say anything until you were finished and I suspect that's just the start of your announcements."

He chuckled. His kid brother knew him all too well. Shaking his head with amusement, he met his brother's happy gaze and continued. "Do you know why I was angry about your planned marriage to Macy?"

"'Cause you wanted her for yourself?" his brother offered, surprising him.

"You knew that?"

"I suspected, but she needed my help—"

"And you were always one to help a friend. Much like Tim helped Macy when she told him she was pregnant," he said, but before he could continue, Jericho jumped in.

"I always thought she and Tim kind of rushed things. Her being pregnant out of wedlock explains—"

"No, it doesn't explain everything, bro. Macy was pregnant with *my* child."

Silence followed for long moments until Jericho plopped forward in his chair and splayed his hands on the top of his desk, his eyes wide and a look of shock on his face.

"T.J. is your son? And you never knew?"

"Never. I suppose you never suspected it," he said and examined his brother's features as the surprise slowly faded from Jericho's face.

"Never. I mean, T.J. didn't look that much like Tim, but I always thought he favored Macy." He paused and shook his head in disbelief.

"You have a son. I have a nephew," he said with a dazed tone in his voice.

"I have a son and yes, you have a nephew. Not to mention that Dad…well, Dad's a granddad."

"And he'll have another grandchild soon. I imagine the old man will be as pleased as a racehorse put out to stud. His family's growing by leaps and bounds," Jericho said and once again shook his head as he thought about everything.

"What do you and Macy plan to do? I mean, you've told T.J., I assume—"

"We have," he said and bounced his joined hands up and down nervously. "He seems to be handling it well. He says he'll do whatever will make his mom happy."

Jericho covered his mouth with one hand, his actions thoughtful as he rubbed his hand across his lips.

"What will make you happy, Fisher?"

"I can't imagine being without Macy again, Jericho. I think I'm going to ask her to marry me."

Jericho let out a small whoop, hurried around the desk and wrapped him up in a powerful bear hug. "I'm glad to hear that, Fisher."

He returned the embrace and when they parted, Jericho sat on the edge of his desk and picked up one of the envelopes there. Holding it up, he said, "Seems like we're not the only ones in a marrying kind of mood."

He held out the fancy off-white envelope and Fisher took it, removed the invite from within—one to Georgie Grady and Nick Sheffield's wedding. The event was barely a week away and he chuckled as he thought about good ol' Georgie Grady finally tying the knot after so many years.

"Seems like Cupid's been busy in Esperanza lately."

Jericho eyeballed him intently. "Are you complaining, big bro?"

He thought about going home to Macy later that day and warmth and happiness filled him.

"Not at all, lil' bro. Not at all," he confessed.

Chapter 25

A week later, they gathered for Georgie and Nick's reception at the local catering hall. The wedding had taken place earlier that day at the church where less than a month before she had planned on marrying Jericho. Where Jericho had married Olivia three weeks ago.

She held Fisher's hand beneath the table where they sat, listening as Clay relayed the information he had been able to obtain about Ryder after visiting the prison.

"The warden wouldn't see me at first, but I insisted. That's when he finally let me into his office and told me that Ryder had died a few months ago," he said and beside him, his wife Tamara covered his hand as it rested on the table and tenderly twined her fingers with his.

When Clay spoke once again, his voice was tight and slightly hoarse from holding back his emotions. "It's hard to believe he's gone. I feel like he's still alive. I still feel as if one day I'll be able to make amends for the distance between us over the last few years."

Jewel, who was sitting beside Jericho and Olivia at the table and her date, Deputy Adam Rawlings, leaned closer as the music from the band grew a little louder, making conversation slightly more difficult. "I know how you feel. When I lost my fiancé and baby…it took a long time for me to really accept that they were gone."

She had experienced the same emotions after Tim's death. For the longest time, she would roll over in bed, expecting him to be there. She would even smell him sometimes and recounted those sentiments in an effort to comfort Clay.

"Tim used to have this funky aftershave that T.J. had bought him for one Father's Day. For months after he was gone I imagined that I could still smell it," she said and Fisher tightened his hold on her hand, offering her solace.

Clay's eyes narrowed at her comment. "I thought I smelled Ryder the other day. He used to smoke these fancy cigarettes that had this weird odor…" His voice trailed off, but then he quickly added, "I think they were like the ones I found by the fence separating the Bar None and the Hopechest Ranch. You have the butts, right, Jericho?"

"I do, Clay. I sent one of them on to the state police for analysis."

"We appreciate you doing that. It'll be nice to know there's no worries to have about the kids," Jewel said and glanced in the direction of a large table at the other side of the room where T.J., Sara and Joe sat together with Georgie's little girl and the other kids from the Hopechest.

"They're having a nice time," her boss said and suddenly the band launched into a Texas two-step.

Jericho stood and pulled his newlywed wife Olivia to her feet. "Come on, darlin'. I've got to teach this city girl how to dance before you get too big to move around."

Macy smiled as Olivia eased into Jericho's arms and the two of them hurried to the dance floor. It pleased her that Jericho seemed so happy and as she shot a glance at Fisher, there was no doubting the contentment on his face. Even Clay, with his sadness over his brother's loss, seemed to have an easier burden with Tamara beside him.

As her gaze skipped to Jewel, she wished her boss would find happiness and as if some fickle Cupid somewhere was listening, Adam leaned toward her and said, "Would you mind taking a spin with me, Miss Jewel?"

To her surprise, Jewel's lips tightened with displeasure. "Thanks, Adam, but I think I'll sit this one out."

The deputy's face went white with anger before flushing red from embarrassment. His jaw clenched tightly, he dipped his head, rose from beside her and walked away to the bar at the side of the room. He stood stiffly while waiting for a drink.

"You okay, Jewel?" she asked.

Her friend shrugged and looked away from the deputy. "There's just something about him lately… I guess I'm a little angry about how he handled everything with Sara and T.J."

She understood completely. She'd had her moments of hostility about the deputy's actions, but she didn't want that to create problems for her friend. "I understand, but don't be mad at him on my account. I kind of thought he had a crush on you."

"Which I guess explains why he asked me to be his date for the wedding, although I'm wondering why I agreed to come with him. I mean, he's nice and everything, but the more I think about it, the better it is to wait for the right person. I mean, just look at Graham Colton over there," she said and motioned to where the older man sat, watching all the goings on, but physically and emotionally alone.

"He never was one to join in, but I think he really did love my mom," Clay said, surprising everyone with his comment.

"Too bad he didn't know how to show it," Fisher said and glanced her way, his gaze hot and intense, leaving no doubt that he knew how to demonstrate his affections for her.

As heat pooled in her center at just how he would show her once they were home, she leaned close to him and whispered a warning. "Fisher, please. You'll have to wait until later."

Jericho and Olivia returned just then, slightly sweaty and winded from their two-step adventure. As Jericho glanced their way, he said, "You two have a secret?"

Fisher chuckled and wrapped an arm around her shoulders. "Actually, it seems as good a time as any to make this announcement—Macy and I are getting married. She and T.J. are going to join me at West Point where I've accepted a teaching position."

Congratulations and hugs erupted all around the table and she found herself going from one person to the other, accepting all their good wishes. She finished making her rounds by going to Jewel, who hugged her hard.

"I'm so happy for you, Macy. Fisher seems like a wonderful man."

"He is," she said and brushed back a lock of her friend's

short light brown hair. "I know that one day, you'll meet a wonderful man, as well."

Jewel grinned and playfully tugged on her hand. "I hope you'll let me be your bridesmaid again."

"Without a doubt. Fisher and I will be setting a date shortly and finalizing all the plans soon. I'll stay as long as you need me at the ranch."

"Don't worry about that. Ana and I can handle things for a little longer," her boss reassured her, but Macy didn't want to leave her in a lurch.

"With Fisher accepting the appointment, we'll have some more time in Esperanza and I'll help you find my replacement. Get things settled at the ranch before I go."

"I'd appreciate that," Jewel said and after, they all sat back down around the table to enjoy the rest of the wedding.

As Fisher took her hand in his again and they shared an intimate glance, she realized that soon they would be gathering to celebrate her wedding to Fisher. Her son…no, their son would be standing beside them, blessing their union. Making them a family finally.

Her secret was out in the open and as she faced Fisher and brought her lips to his, she whispered, "Are you sure?"

His grin erupted against her mouth, calming any of her fears. "I'm sure that our being together is about eighteen years overdue. And you?"

She chuckled against his lips and said, "I'm sure that if I do want I want to right now, Jericho will have to lock us up."

He joined in her laughter and closed the distance to her lips, kissing her deeply until an amused cough drove them apart.

"Bro, I think it's time you and Macy went home," Jericho said, his eyebrow arched in amusement.

Fisher jumped to his feet, her hand in his. "For once, I'm not going to argue with you."

The deputy's patrol car had passed him along the edge of the road, but he had flattened himself to the ground in a small ditch and gone unseen. When the car returned on its rounds and skipped by him on its way back to town, he waited for a few more minutes before rising from the ditch and making the nearly mile long trek to the cut in the fence.

He moved swiftly and quietly, slipped through the cut barbed wire on his way to the small stand of trees and the caves where he and Clay had played as kids.

Clay, he thought, thinking about his older brother and how he had looked the other day when he had come out to inspect the area and noticed the cut in the fence.

Ryder had been hiding by the trees, watching him. Wanting to reach out and let Clay know he was there, but he couldn't do it just yet.

He paused by the fence along the edge of the Bar None and Hopechest, glanced down toward Esperanza. He had noticed the traffic around the church earlier in the day and later, the gathering of cars and people at the one big hall in town.

Another wedding in Esperanza.

There seemed to be a lot of them lately and he wondered who was getting married today. Wondered whether any of the people at the wedding were aware of what was happening right beneath their noses.

Of course not, he told himself, pushing away from the fence and heading toward the caves. Not even the sheriff had a clue about what was going on or that the big bad little brother was back to get to the bottom of it. To redeem himself for all the wrong that he had done as a young man. The wrong that had driven a wedge between himself and his older brother Clay.

As he paused at the edge of the trees, he looked back toward town again and smiled at the thought of returning home.

"Soon," Ryder told himself and slipped into one of the caves, intent on completing his redemption.

Jericho and Fisher waited on the steps of the church, T.J. beside them much as they had stood there nearly a month earlier. Only there was no doubt now about who Macy was wedding and that this would be a real marriage.

Clasping his hands before him tightly, he rocked back and forth on his heels, prompting T.J. to ask, "Are you nervous?"

Nervous. Excited. Happy.

"I am," he confessed and examined his son. "Are you?"

T.J. shrugged, but the fabric of his dress blue suit barely moved since the jacket was slightly big on him. Not for long, he knew, thinking back on how both he and Jericho had filled out in their senior year.

Clapping a hand on T.J.'s shoulder, he said, "I'm glad we'll have the time to get to know each other."

"I'm glad, too," T.J. responded.

A second later, a limo pulled up in front of the church. Jewel stepped out first, looking beautiful in a pale pink bridesmaid's dress that hugged her slender figure. As she noticed them waiting on the steps of the church, she waved at them.

"Time for you to head inside. It's bad luck to see the bride before the wedding," she called out in warning, but before they could take a step, Macy slipped from the limo.

The dress she wore this time was nothing like the one she had purchased for her wedding to Jericho. This one was …

Amazing, he thought, taking note of the intricate skirt of the pale ice blue dress with its yards and yards of palest white lace. The bodice hugged her curves, accentuating her tempting shape and her shoulders were bare, making him want to touch her.

As his gaze skimmed up to her face and hair, he realized that she had gone all out. Makeup expertly done and her shoulder length brown hair stylishly cut and set in a tousled style that screamed sexy.

"Fisher?" his brother prompted.

He faced him and T.J., blushed as he saw the look on his brother's face and T.J.'s amused look as he said, "Aw, come on, Fisher. That's my mom."

"She's beautiful, isn't she?" he said and with a wink at Macy, he once again clapped T.J. on the back.

"Ready to become a family?"

T.J. shot a quick hesitant look back at his mom, but then a wide grin erupted on his face. "You love her, don't you?"

"I do. With all my heart."

"Then I guess it's okay," T.J. said. "I'll go get Mom."

Fisher watched as he walked away, went to Macy's side and slipped his arm through hers.

He was about to head into the church when T.J. shouted, "Wait up, Fisher."

To his surprise, T.J. hurried Macy over and then slipped his arm through Fisher's. "A family, right?" T.J. said as he stood between them.

He met Macy's gaze which was shimmering with tears of happiness. Grinning, he said, "A family, T.J."

Looking up at Jericho, who was waiting beside Jewel, he said, "Come on, bro. The three of us have places to go."

As they followed Jewel and Jericho down the aisle of the

church, he felt the secrets of the past slip away, replaced by the excitement of his new tour of duty—building a life with Macy and T.J.

It was a mission he knew would bring nothing but happiness for the three of them.

* * * * *

*Don't miss the next book in this
exciting series: BABY'S WATCH by Justine Davis,
available January 2009.*

Silhouette Desire kicks off 2009 with
MAN OF THE MONTH, *a yearlong program
featuring incredible heroes by stellar authors.*

When navy SEAL Hunter Cabot returns home for some
much-needed R & R, he discovers he's a married man.
There's just one problem: he's never met his "bride."

Enjoy this sneak peek at Maureen Child's
AN OFFICER AND A MILLIONAIRE.
Available January 2009 from Silhouette Desire.

One

Hunter Cabot, Navy SEAL, had a healing bullet wound in his side, thirty days' leave and, apparently, a wife he'd never met.

On the drive into his hometown of Springville, California, he stopped for gas at Charlie Evans's service station. That's where the trouble started.

"Hunter! Man, it's good to see you! Margie didn't tell us you were coming home."

"Margie?" Hunter leaned back against the front fender of his black pickup truck and winced as his side gave a small twinge of pain. Silently then, he watched as the man he'd known since high school filled his tank.

Charlie grinned, shook his head and pumped gas. "Guess your wife was lookin' for a little 'alone' time with you, huh?"

"My—" Hunter couldn't even say the word. *Wife?* He didn't have a wife. "Look, Charlie..."

"Don't blame her, of course," his friend said with a wink as he finished up and put the gas cap back on. "You being gone all the time with the SEALs must be hard on the ol' love life."

He'd never had any complaints, Hunter thought, frowning at the man still talking a mile a minute. "What're you—"

"Bet Margie's anxious to see you. She told us all about that R and R trip you two took to Bali." Charlie's dark brown eyebrows lifted and wiggled.

"Charlie..."

"Hey, it's okay, you don't have to say a thing, man."

What the hell could he say? Hunter shook his head, paid for his gas and as he left, told himself Charlie was just losing it. Maybe the guy had been smelling gas fumes too long.

But as it turned out, it wasn't just Charlie. Stopped at a red light on Main Street, Hunter glanced out his window to smile at Mrs. Harker, his second-grade teacher who was now at least a hundred years old. In the middle of the crosswalk, the old lady stopped and shouted, "Hunter Cabot, you've got yourself a wonderful wife. I hope you appreciate her."

Scowling now, he only nodded at the old woman—the only teacher who'd ever scared the crap out of him. What the hell was going on here? Was everyone but him nuts?

His temper beginning to boil, he put up with a few more comments about his "wife" on the drive through town before finally pulling into the wide, circular drive leading to the Cabot mansion. Hunter didn't have a clue what was going on, but he planned to get to the bottom of it. Fast.

He grabbed his duffel bag, stalked into the house and paid no attention to the housekeeper, who ran at him, fluttering both hands. "Mr. Hunter!"

"Sorry, Sophie," he called out over his shoulder as he took the stairs two at a time. "Need a shower, then we'll talk."

He marched down the long, carpeted hallway to the rooms that were always kept ready for him. In his suite, Hunter tossed the duffel down and stopped dead. The shower in his bathroom was running. His *wife?*

Anger and curiosity boiled in his gut, creating a churning mass that had him moving forward without even thinking about it. He opened the bathroom door to a wall of steam and the sound of a woman singing—off-key. Margie, no doubt.

Well, if she was his wife... Hunter walked across the room, yanked the shower door open and stared in at a curvy, naked, temptingly wet woman.

She whirled to face him, slapping her arms across her naked body while she gave a short, terrified scream.

Hunter smiled. "Hi, honey. I'm home."

* * * * *

Be sure to look for
AN OFFICER AND A MILLIONAIRE
by USA TODAY *bestselling author Maureen Child.*
Available January 2009 from Silhouette Desire.

nocturne™

MICHELE HAUF

THE DEVIL TO PAY

Bewitching the Dark

Vampire phoenix Ivan Drake's soul belonged
to the Devil Himself, and he had no choice but
to enforce Himself's wicked law. But when Ivan
was sent to claim the *Book of All Spells* for his
master, he wasn't prepared for his encounter
with the book's enchanting protector. With his
soul already the property of another, would he be
willing to lose his heart, as well?

Available January 2009 wherever books are sold.

www.eHarlequin.com
www.paranormalromanceblog.com

SN61802

Silhouette
Romantic
SUSPENSE

COMING NEXT MONTH

#1543 BOUNTY HUNTER'S WOMAN—Linda Turner
Broken Arrow Ranch
Hired as her bodyguard, bounty hunter Donovan Jones hasn't even met Priscilla Wyatt before she's kidnapped and he has to rescue her. Priscilla is wary of Donovan's true intentions, but she'll have to learn to put her life—and her heart—in his hands if she wants to save her family's ranch in time.

#1544 BABY'S WATCH—Justine Davis
The Coltons: Family First
Former bad boy Ryder Colton has never felt a connection to much, so he's shocked when he feels one to the baby he helps deliver, as well as her mother. Ana Morales doesn't quite trust this stranger, but when her daughter is taken by a smuggling ring, she teams up with him to rescue the baby. Will they put their lives on the line for love?

#1545 TERMS OF ENGAGEMENT—Kylie Brant
Alpha Squad
On the run from a hit man, Lindsay Bradford's bravery in a hostage situation puts her picture on the news, and now she must flee again. But after they share a passionate night, Detective Jack Langley won't let her go. She never thought she'd trust another cop to help her, but Lindsay finally risks everything when she puts her trust in Jack....

#1546 BURNING SECRETS—Elizabeth Sinclair
When forest ranger Jesse Kingston is sent on forced leave after his best friend dies in a firestorm, he returns home to find himself face-to-face with Karen Ellis—the woman who's carrying his friend's baby. Both suspicious about the man's death, they join together to discover the truth—about the fire and about their hearts' deepest desires.